DIAMOND IN THE ROUGH

Center Point
Large Print

Also by Diana Palmer
Available from Center Point Large Print

Circle of Gold
Blind Promises
Boss Man
Heartbreaker
Lawman
Winter Roses
Iron Cowboy
Heart of Stone

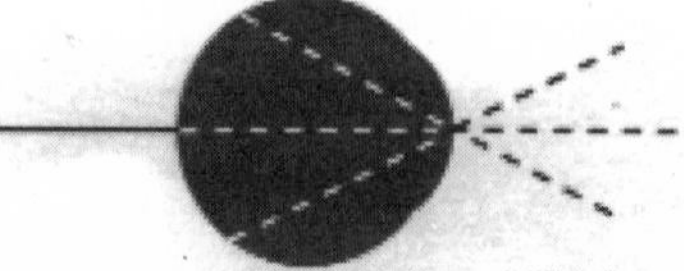

Diamond in the Rough

Diana Palmer

Center Point Publishing
Thorndike, Maine

This Center Point Large Print edition
is published in the year 2009 by arrangement with
Harlequin Books S.A.

The text of this Large Print edition is unabridged.
In other aspects, this book may vary
from the original edition.
Printed in the United States of America.
Set in 16-point Times New Roman type.

ISBN: 978-1-60285-515-1

Library of Congress Cataloging-in-Publication Data

Palmer, Diana.
Diamond in the rough / Diana Palmer. -- Center Point large print ed.
p. cm.
ISBN 978-1-60285-515-1 (large print : lib. bdg.)
1. Millionaires--Fiction. 2. Ranchers--Fiction. 3. Montana--Fiction.
4. Large type books. I. Title.

PS3566.A513D536 2009
813'.54--dc22

2009016710

For my friend Nancy C.,
who came all the way from Indiana
just to meet me.
Thanks for the beautiful cowboy quilt, Nancy—
I'll never forget you!

And thanks to all of you on my bulletin board at my Web site, including Nancy and Amy, who spent hours of their precious free time making me a compendium of all the families in Jacobsville, Texas! Now, guys, maybe I can make fewer mistakes when I write about them! Love you all.

CHAPTER ONE

THE little town, Hollister, wasn't much bigger than Medicine Ridge, Montana, where John Callister and his brother Gil had a huge ranch. But they'd decided that it wasn't wise to confine their whole livelihood to one area. They needed to branch out a little, maybe try something different. On the main ranch, they ran a purebred bull and breeding operation with state-of-the-art science. John and Gil had decided to try something new here in Hollister, Montana; a ranch which would deal specifically in young purebred sale bulls, using the latest technology to breed for specific traits like low calving weight, lean conformation, and high weight gain ratio, among others. In addition, they were going to try new growth programs that combined specific organic grasses with mixed protein and grains to improve their production.

In the depressed economy, tailor-made beef cattle would cater to the discerning organic beef consumer. Gil and John didn't run beef cattle, but their champion bulls were bred to appeal to ranchers who did. It was a highly competitive field, especially with production costs going sky-high. Cattlemen could no longer depend on random breeding programs left up to nature. These days, progeny resulted from tailored genetics. It was a high-tech sort of agriculture. Gil and John had pioneered some of the newer computer-based programs that yielded high on profits coupled with less wasteful producer strategies.

For example, Gil had heard about a program that used methane gas from cattle waste to produce energy to run ranch equipment. The initial expense for the hardware had been high, but it was already producing results. Much of the electricity used to light the barns and power the ranch equipment was due to the new technology. Any surplus energy could be sold back to the electric company. The brothers had also installed solar panels to heat water in the main house and run hydraulic equipment in the breeding barn and the stockyard. One of the larger agricultural magazines had featured an article about their latest innovations. Gil's photo, and that of his daughters and his new wife had graced the pages of the trade publication. John had been at a cattle show and missed the photo shoot. He didn't mind. He'd never been one to court publicity. Nor was Gil. But they wouldn't miss a chance to advertise their genetically superior cattle.

John usually traveled to show the cattle. But he was getting tired of spending his life on the road. Now that Gil had married Kasie, the brothers' former secretary, and the small girls from Gil's first marriage, Bess and Jenny, were in school, John was feeling lonelier than ever, and more restless. Not that he'd had a yen for Kasie, but Gil's remarriage made him aware of the passing of time. He wasn't getting any younger; he was in his thirties. The traveling was beginning to wear on him. Although he dated infrequently, he'd never found a woman he wanted to keep. He was also feeling like a fifth wheel at the family ranch.

So he'd volunteered to come up to Hollister to rebuild this small, dilapidated cattle ranch that he and Gil had purchased and see if an injection of capital and new blood stock and high-tech innovation could bring it from bankruptcy to a higher status in the world of purebred cattle.

The house, which John had only seen from aerial photos, was a wreck. No maintenance had been done on it for years by its elderly owner. He'd had to let most of his full-time cowboys go when the market fell, and he wasn't able to keep up with the demands of the job with the part-timers he retained. Fences got broken, cattle escaped, the well went dry, the barn burned down and, finally, the owner decided to cut his losses. He'd offered the ranch for sale, as-is, and the Callister brothers had bought it from him. The old man had gone back East to live with a daughter.

Now John had a firsthand look at the monumental task facing him. He'd have to hire new cowboys, build a barn as well as a stable, spend a few thousand making the house livable, sink a well, restring the fences, buy equipment, set up the methane-based power production plant . . . He groaned at the thought of it. The ranch in Medicine Ridge was state-of-the-art. This was medieval, by comparison. It was going to take longer than a month or two. This was a job that would take many months. And all that work had to be done before any cattle could be brought onto the place. What had seemed like a pleasant hobby in the beginning now looked like it would become a career.

There were two horses in a corral with a lean-to for protection from the weather, all that remained of the old man's Appaloosas. The remuda, or string of working ranch horses, had been sold off long ago. The remaining part-time cowboys told John that they'd brought their own mounts with them to work, while there was still a herd of cattle on the place. But the old man had sold off all his stock and let the part-timers go before he sold the ranch. Lucky, John thought, that he'd been able to track them down and offer them full-time jobs again. They were eager for the work. The men all lived within a radius of a few miles. If John had to wait on replacing the ranch's horses, the men could bring their own to work temporarily while John restocked the place.

He planned to rebuild and restock quickly. Something would have to be done about a barn. A place for newborn calves and sick cattle was his first priority. That, and the house. He was sleeping on the floor in a sleeping bag, heating water on a camp stove for shaving and bathing in the creek.

Thank God, he thought, that it was spring and not winter. Food was purchased in the town's only café, where he had two meals a day. He ate sandwiches for lunch, purchased from a cooler in the convenience store/gas station at the edge of town. It was rough living for a man who was used to five-star hotels and the best food money could buy. But it was his choice, he reminded himself.

He drove into town in a mid-level priced pickup truck. No use advertising that he was wealthy. Prices would skyrocket, since he wasn't on friendly terms with anyone here. He'd only met the cowboys. The people in town didn't even know his name yet.

The obvious place to start, he reasoned, was the feed store. It sold ranch supplies including tack. The owner might know where he could find a reputable builder.

He pulled up at the front door and strode in. The place was dusty and not well-kept. There seemed to be only one employee, a slight girl with short, wavy dark hair and a pert figure, wearing a knit pullover with worn jeans and boots.

She was sorting bridles but she looked up when he approached. Like many old-time cowboys, he was sporting boots with spurs that jingled when he walked. He was also wearing an old Colt .45 in a holster slung low on his hip under the open denim shirt he was wearing with jeans and a black T-shirt. It was wild country, this part of Montana, and he wasn't going out on the range without some way of protecting himself from potential predators.

The girl stared at him in an odd, fixed way. He didn't realize that he had the looks that would have been expected in a motion picture star. His blond hair, under the wide-brimmed cowboy hat, had a sheen like gold, and his handsome face was very attractive. He had the tall, elegant body of a rider, lean and fit and muscular without exaggerated lines.

"What the hell are you doing?" came a gruff, angry voice from the back. "I told you to go bring in those new sacks of feed before the rain ruins them, not play with the tack! Get your lazy butt moving, girl!"

The girl flushed, looking frightened. "Yes, sir," she said at once, and jumped up to do what he'd told her to.

John didn't like the way the man spoke to her. She was very young, probably still in her teens. No man should speak that way to a child.

He approached the man with a deadpan expression, only his blue eyes sparkling with temper.

The man, overweight and half-bald, older than John, turned as he approached. "Something I can do for you?" he asked in a bored tone, as if he didn't care whether he got the business or not.

"You the owner?" John asked him.

The man glared. "The manager. Tarleton. Bill Tarleton."

John tilted his hat back. "I need to find someone who can build a barn."

The manager's eyebrows arched. His eyes slid over John's worn jeans and boots and inexpensive clothing. He laughed. His expression was an insult. "You own a ranch around here?" he asked in disbelief.

John fought back his temper. "My boss does," he said, in an impulsive moment. "He's hiring. He just bought the Bradbury place out on Chambers Road."

"That old place?" Tarleton made a face. "Hell, it's a wreck! Bradbury just sat on his butt and let the place go to hell. Nobody understood why. He had some good cattle years ago, cattlemen came from as far away as Oklahoma and Kansas to buy his stock."

"He got old," John said.

"I guess. A barn, you say." He pursed his lips. "Well, Jackson Hewett has a construction business. He builds houses. Fancy houses, some of them. I reckon he could build a barn. He lives just outside town, over by the old train station. He's in the local telephone directory."

"I'm obliged," John said.

"Your boss . . . he'll be needing feed and tack, I guess?" Tarleton added.

John nodded.

"If I don't have it on hand, I can order it."

"I'll keep that in mind. I need something right now, though—a good tool kit."

“Sassy!” he yelled. “The man wants a tool kit! Bring one of the boxes from that new line we started stocking!”

“Yes, sir!” There was the sound of scrambling boots.

“She ain’t much help,” the manager grumbled. “Misses work sometimes. Got a mother with cancer and a little sister, six, that the mother adopted. I guess she’ll end up alone, just her and the kid.”

“Does the mother get government help?” John asked, curious.

“Not much,” Tarleton scoffed. “They say she never did much except sit with sick folk, even before she got the cancer. Sassy’s bringing in the only money they got. The old man took off years ago with another woman. Just left. At least they got a house. Ain’t much of one, but it’s a roof over their heads. The mother got it in the divorce settlement.”

John felt a pang when he noticed the girl tugging a heavy toolbox. She looked as if she was barely able to lift a bridle.

“Here, I’ll take that,” John said, trying to sound nonchalant. He took it from her hands and set it on the counter, popping it open. His eyebrows lifted as he examined the tools. “Nice.”

“Expensive, too, but it’s worth it,” Tarleton told him.

“Boss wants to set up an account in his own name, but I’ll pay cash for this,” John said, pulling out his wallet. "He gave me pocket money for essentials."

Tarleton's eyes got bigger as John started peeling off twenty-dollar bills. "Okay. What name do I put on the account?"

"Callister," John told him without batting an eyelash. "Gil Callister."

"Hey, I've heard of him," Tarleton said at once, giving John a bad moment. "He's got a huge ranch down in Medicine Ridge."

"That's the one," John said. "Ever seen him?"

"Who, me?" The older man laughed. "I don't run in those circles, no, sir. We're just country folk here, not millionaires."

John felt a little less worried. It would be to his advantage if the locals didn't know who he really was. Not yet, anyway. Since he was having to give up cattle shows for the foreseeable future, there wasn't much chance that his face would be gracing any trade papers. It might be nice, he pondered, to be accepted as an ordinary man for once. His wealth seemed to draw opportunists, especially feminine ones. He could enjoy playing the part of a cowboy for a change.

"No problem with opening an account here, then, if we put some money down first as a credit?" John asked.

"No problem at all." Tarleton grinned. "I'll start that account right now. You tell Mr. Callister anything he needs, I can get for him!"

"I'll tell him."

"And your name . . . ?" the manager asked.

"John," he replied. "John Taggert."

Taggert was his middle name. His maternal grandfather, a pioneer in South Dakota, had that name.

"Taggert." The manager shook his head. "Never heard that one."

John smiled. "It's not famous."

The girl was still standing beside the counter. John handed her the bills to pay for the toolbox. She worked the cash register and counted out his change.

"Thanks," John said, smiling at her.

She smiled back at him, shyly. Her green eyes were warm and soft. "You're welcome."

"Get back to work," Tarleton told her.

"Yes, sir." She turned and went back to the bags on the loading platform.

John frowned. "Isn't she too slight to be hefting bags that size?"

"It goes with the job," Tarleton said defensively. "I had a strong teenage boy working for me, but his parents moved to Billings and he had to go along. She was all I could get. She swore she could do the job. So I'm letting her."

"I guess she's stronger than she looks," John remarked, but he didn't like it.

Tarleton nodded absently. He was putting Gil Callister's name in his ledger.

"I'll be back," John told him as he picked up the toolbox.

Tarleton nodded again.

John glanced at the girl, who was straining over a heavy bag, and walked out of the store with a scowl on his face.

He paused. He didn't know why. He glanced back into the store and saw the manager standing on the loading platform, watching the girl lift the feed sacks. It wasn't the look a manager should be giving an employee. John's eyes narrowed. He was going to do something about that.

One of the older cowboys, Chad Dean by name, was waiting for him at the house when he brought in the toolbox.

"Say, that's a nice one," he told the other man. "Your boss must be stinking rich."

"He is," John mused. "Pays good, too."

The cowboy chuckled. "That would be nice, getting a paycheck that I could feed my kids on. I couldn't move my family to another town without giving up land that belonged to my grandfather, so I toughed it out. It's been rough, what with food prices and gas going through the roof."

"You'll get your regular check plus travel expenses," John told him. "We'll pay for the gas if we have to send you anywhere to pick up things."

"That's damned considerate."

"If you work hard, your wages will go up."

"We'll all work hard," Dean promised solemnly. "We're just happy to have jobs."

John pursed his lips. "Do you know a girl named Sassy? Works for Tarleton in the feed store?"

"Yeah," Dean replied tersely. "He's married, and he makes passes at Sassy. She needs that job. Her mama's dying. There's a six-year-old kid lives with them, too, and Sassy has to take care of her. I don't know how in hell she manages on what she gets paid. All that, and having to put up with Tarleton's harassment, too. My wife told her she should call the law and report him. She won't. She says she can't afford to lose the position. Town's so small, she'd never get hired again. Tarleton would make sure of it, just for spite, if she quit."

John nodded. His eyes narrowed thoughtfully. "I expect things will get easier for her," he predicted.

"Do you? Wish I did. She's a sweet kid. Always doing things for other people." He smiled. "My son had his appendix out. It was Sassy who saw what it was, long before we did. He was in the feed store when he got sick. She called the doctor. He looked over my Mark and agreed it was appendicitis. Doc drove the boy over to Billings to the hospital. Sassy went to see him. God knows how she got there. Her old beat-up vehicle would never make it as far as Billings. Hitched a ride with Carl Parks, I expect. He's in his seventies, but he watches out for Sassy and her mother. Good old fellow."

John nodded. "Sounds like it." He hesitated. "How old is the girl?"

"Eighteen or nineteen, I guess. Just out of high school."

"I figured that." John was disappointed. He didn't understand why. "Okay, here's what we're going to do about those fences temporarily . . ."

In the next two days, John did some amateur detective work. He phoned a private detective who worked for the Callisters on business deals and put him on the Tarleton man. It didn't take him long to report back.

The feed store manager had been allowed to resign from a job in Billings for unknown reasons, but the detective found one other employee who said it was sexual harassment of an employee. He wasn't charged with anything. He'd moved here, to Hollister, with his family when the owner of the feed store, a man named Jake McGuire, advertised in a trade paper for someone to manage it for him. Apparently Tarleton had been the only applicant and McGuire was desperate. Tarleton got the job.

"This McGuire," John asked over his cell phone, "how old is he?"

"In his thirties," came the reply. "Everyone I spoke to about him said that he's a decent sort."

"In other words, he doesn't have a clue that Tarleton's hassling the girl."

"That would be my guess."

John's eyes twinkled. "Do you suppose McGuire would like to sell that business?"

There was a chuckle. "He's losing money hand over fist on that place. Two of the people I spoke to said he'd almost give it away to get rid of it."

"Thanks," John said. "That answers my question. Can you get me McGuire's telephone number?"

"Already did. Here it is."

John wrote it down. The next morning, he put in a call to McGuire Enterprises in Billings.

"I'm looking to buy a business in a town called Hollister," John said after he'd introduced himself. "Someone said you might know the owner of the local feed store."

"The feed store?" McGuire replied. "You want to buy it?" He sounded astonished.

"I might," John said. "If the price is right."

There was a pause. "Okay, here's the deal. That business was started by my father over forty years ago. I inherited it when he died. I don't really want to sell it."

"It's going bankrupt," John replied.

There was another pause. "Yeah, I know," came the disgusted reply. "I had to put in a new manager there, and he didn't come cheap. I had to move him and his wife from Billings down here." He sighed. "I'm between a rock and a hard place. I own several businesses, and I don't have the time to manage them myself. That particular one has sentimental value. The manager just went to work. There's a chance he can pull it out of the red."

"There's a better chance that he's going to get you involved in a major lawsuit."

"What? What for?"

"For one thing, he was let go from his last job for sexual harassment, or that's what we turned up on a background check. He's up to his old tricks in Hollister, this time with a young girl just out of high school that he hired to work for him."

"Good Lord! He came with excellent references!"

"He might have them," John said. "But it wouldn't surprise me if that wasn't the first time he lost a job for the same reason. He was giving the girl the eye when I was in there. There's local gossip that the girl may sue if your manager doesn't lay off her. There goes your bottom line," he added dryly.

"Well, that's what you get when you're desperate for personnel," McGuire said wearily. "I couldn't find anybody else who'd take the job. I can't fire him without proper cause, and I just paid to move him there! What a hell of a mess!"

"You don't want to sell the business. Okay. How about leasing it to us? We'll fire Tarleton on the grounds that we're leasing the business, put in a manager of our own, and you'll make money. We'll have you in the black in two months."

"And just who is 'we'?" McGuire wanted to know.

“My brother and I. We’re ranchers.”

“But why would you want to lease a feed store in the middle of nowhere?”

“Because we just bought the Bradbury place. We’re going to rebuild the house, add a stable and a barn, and we’re going to raise purebred young bulls on the place. The feed store is going to do a lot of business when we start adding personnel to the outfit.”

“Old man Bradbury and my father were best friends,” McGuire reminisced. “He was a fine rancher, a nice gentleman. His health failed and the business failed with him. It’s nice to know it will be a working ranch again.”

“It’s good land. We’ll make it pay.”

“What did you say your name was?”

“Callister,” John told him. “My brother and I have a sizable spread over in Medicine Ridge.”

“Those Callisters? My God, your holdings are worth millions!”

“At least.” John chuckled.

There was a soft whistle. “Well, if you’re going to keep me in orders, I suppose I’d be willing to lease the place to you.”

“And the manager?”

“I just moved him there,” McGuire groaned again.

“We’ll pay to move him back to Billings and give him two weeks severance pay,” John said. “I will not agree to let him stay on,” he added firmly.

"He may sue."

"Let him," John replied tersely. "If he tries it, I'll make it my life's work to see that any skeleton in his past is brought into the light of day. You can tell him that."

"I'll tell him."

"If you'll give me your attorney's name and number, I'll have our legal department contact him," John said. "I think we'll get along."

There was a deep chuckle. "So do I."

"There's one other matter."

"Yes?"

John hesitated. "I'm going to be working on the place myself, but I don't want anyone local to know who I am. I'll be known as the ranch foreman—Taggert by name. Got that?"

There was a chuckle. "Keeping it low-key, I see. Sure. I won't blow your cover."

"Especially to Tarleton and his employee," John emphasized.

"No problem. I'll tell him your boss phoned me."

"I'm much obliged."

"Before we settle this deal, do you have someone in mind who can take over the business in two weeks if I put Tarleton on notice?"

"Indeed I do," John replied. "He's a retired corporate executive who's bored stiff with retirement. Mind like a steel trap. He could make money in the desert."

"Sounds like just the man for the job."

"I'll have him up here in two weeks."

"That's a deal, then."

"We'll talk again when the paperwork goes through."

"Yes."

John hung up. He felt better about the girl. Not that he expected Tarleton to quit the job without a fight. He hoped the threat of uncovering any past sins would work the magic. The thought of Sassy being bothered by that would-be Casanova was disturbing.

He phoned the architect and asked him to come over to the ranch the following day to discuss drawing up plans for a stable and a barn. He hired an electrician to rewire the house and do the work in the new construction. He employed six new cowboys and an engineer. He set up payroll for everyone he'd hired through the corporation's main offices in Medicine Ridge, and went about getting fences repaired and wells drilled. He also phoned Gil and had him send down a team of engineers to start construction on solar panels to help provide electricity for the operation.

Once those plans were underway, he made a trip into Hollister to see how things were going at the feed store. His detective had managed to dig up three other harassment charges against Tarleton from places he'd lived before he moved to Montana in the first place. There were no convictions, sadly. But the charges might be enough. Armed with that information, he wasn't uncomfortable having words with the man, if it was necessary.

And it seemed that it would be. The minute he walked in the door, he knew there was going to be trouble. Tarleton was talking to a customer, but he gave John a glare that spoke volumes. He finished his business with the customer and waited until he left. Then he walked up to John belligerently.

"What the hell did your employer tell my boss?" he demanded furiously. "He said he was leasing the store, but only on the condition that I didn't go with the deal!"

"Not my problem," John said, and his pale eyes glittered. "It was my boss's decision."

"Well, he's got no reason to fire me!" Tarleton said, his round face flushing. "I'll sue the hell out of him, and your damned boss, too!"

John stepped closer to the man and leaned down, emphasizing his advantage in height. "You're welcome. My boss will go to the local district attorney in Billings and turn over the court documents from your last sexual harassment charge."

Tarleton's face went from red to white in seconds. He froze in place. "He'll . . . what?" he asked weakly.

John's chiseled lips pulled up into a cold smile. "And I'll encourage your hired girl over there—" he indicated her with a jerk of his head "—to come clean about the way you've treated her as well. I think she could be persuaded to bring charges."

Tarleton's arrogance vanished. He looked hunted.

"Take my advice," John said quietly. "Get out while you still have time. My boss won't hesitate a second. He has two daughters of his own." His eyes narrowed menacingly. "One of our ranch hands back home tried to wrestle a temporary maid down in the hay out in our barn. He's serving three to five for sexual assault." John smiled. "We have a firm of attorneys on retainer."

"We?" Tarleton stammered.

"I'm a managerial employee of the ranch. The ranch is a corporation," John replied smoothly.

Tarleton's teeth clenched. "So I guess I'm fired."

"I guess you volunteered to resign," John corrected. "That gets you moved back to Billings at the ranch's expense, and gives you severance pay. It also spares you lawsuits and other . . . difficulties."

The older man weighed his options. John could see his mind working. Tarleton gave John an arrogant look. "What the hell," he said coldly. "I didn't want to live in this damned fly trap anyway!"

He turned on his heel and walked away. The girl, Sassy, was watching the byplay with open curiosity. John raised an eyebrow. She flushed and went back to work at once.

CHAPTER TWO

CASSANDRA PEALE told herself that the intense conversation the new foreman of the Bradbury place was having with her boss didn't concern her. The foreman had made that clear with a lifted eyebrow and a haughty look. But there had been an obvious argument and both men had glanced at her while they were having it. She was worried. She couldn't afford to lose her job. Not when her mother, dying of lung cancer, and her mother's ward, Selene, who was only six, depended on what she brought home so desperately.

She gnawed on a fingernail. They were mostly all chewed off. Her mother was sixty-three, Cassandra, who everyone called Sassy, having been born very late in life. They'd had a ranch until her father had become infatuated with a young waitress at the local cafeteria. He'd left his family and run away with the woman, taking most of their savings with him. Without money to pay bills, Sassy's mother had been forced to sell the cattle and most of the land and let the cowboys go. One of them, little Selene's father, had gotten drunk out of desperation and ran his truck off into the river. They'd found him the next morning, dead, leaving Selene completely alone in the world.

My life, Sassy thought, *is a soap opera*. It even has a villain. She glanced covertly at Mr. Tarleton.

All he needed was a black mustache and a gun. He'd made her working life hell. He knew she couldn't afford to quit. He was always bumping into her "accidentally," trying to handle her. She was sickened by his advances. She'd never even had a boyfriend. The school she'd gone to, in this tiny town, had been a one-room schoolhouse with all ages included and one teacher. There had only been two boys her own age and three girls including Sassy. The other girls were pretty. So Sassy had never been asked out at all. Once, when she was in her senior year of high school, a teacher's visiting nephew had been kind to her, but her mother had been violently opposed to letting her go on a date with a man she didn't know well. It hadn't mattered. Sassy had never felt those things her romance novels spoke of in such enticing and heart-pattering terms. She'd never even been kissed in a grown-up way. Her only sexual experience—if you could call it that—was being physically harassed by that repulsive would-be Romeo standing behind the counter.

She finished dusting the shelves and wished fate would present her with a nice, handsome boss who was single and found her fascinating. She'd have gladly settled for the Bradbury place's new ramrod. But he didn't look as if he found anything about her that attracted him. In fact, he was ignoring her. Story of my life, she thought as she put aside the dust cloth. It was just as well. She had two dependents and no spare time. Where would she fit a man into her desperate life?

"Missed a spot."

She whirled. She flushed as she looked way up into dancing blue eyes. "W . . . what?"

John chuckled. The women in his world were sophisticated and full of easy wisdom. This little violet was as unaffected by the modern world as the store she worked in. He was entranced by her.

"I said you missed a spot." He leaned closer. "It was a joke."

"Oh." She laughed shyly, glancing at the shelf. "I might have missed several, I guess. I can't reach high and there's no ladder."

He smiled. "There's always a soapbox."

"No, no," she returned with a smile. "If I get on one of those, I have to give a political speech."

He groaned. "Don't say those words," he said. "If I have to hear one more comment about the presidential race, I'm having my ears plugged."

"It does get a little irritating, doesn't it?" she asked. "We don't watch the news as much since the television got hit by lightning. The color's gone whacky. I have to think it's a happy benefit of a sad accident."

His eyebrows arched. "Why don't you get a new one?"

She glowered at him. "Because the hardware store doesn't have a fifty-cent one," she said.

It took a minute for that to sink in. John, who

thought nothing of laying down his gold card for the newest plasma wide screened TV, hadn't realized that even a small set was beyond the means of many lower-income people.

He grimaced. "Sorry," he said. "I guess I've gotten too used to just picking up anything I like in stores."

"They don't arrest you for that?" she asked with a straight face, but her twinkling eyes gave her away.

He laughed. "Not so far. I meant," he added, thinking fast, "that my boss pays me a princely salary for my organizational skills."

"He must, if you can afford a new TV," she sighed. "I don't suppose he needs a professional duster?"

"We could ask him."

She shook her head. "I'd rather work here, in a job I do know." She glanced with apprehension at her boss, who was glaring toward the two of them. "I'd better get back to work before he fires me."

"He can't."

She blinked. "He can't what?"

"Fire you," he said quietly. "He's being replaced in two weeks by a new manager."

Her heart stopped. She felt sick. "Oh, dear."

"You won't convince me that you'll miss him," John said curtly.

She bit a fingernail that was already almost gone. "It's not that. A new manager might not want me to work here anymore . . ."

"He will."

She frowned. "How can you know that?"

He pursed his lips. "Because the new manager works for my boss, and my boss said not to change employees."

Her face started to relax. "Really?"

"Really."

She glanced again at Tarleton and felt uncomfortable at the furious glare he gave her. "Oh, dear, did somebody say something to your boss about him . . . about him being forward with me?" she asked worriedly.

"They might have," he said noncommittally.

"He'll get even," she said under her breath. "He's that sort. He told a lie on a customer who was rude to him, about the man's wife. She almost lost her job over it."

John felt his blood rise. "All you have to do is get through the next two weeks," he told her. "If you have a problem with him, any problem, you can call me. I don't care when or what time." He started to pull out his wallet and give her his business card, until he realized that she thought he was pretending to be hired help, not the big boss. "Have you got a pen and paper?" he asked instead.

"In fact, I do," she replied. She moved behind the counter, tore a piece of brown paper off a roll, and picked up a marking pencil. She handed them to him.

He wrote down the number and handed it back to

her. “Don’t be afraid of him,” he added curtly. “He’s in enough trouble without making more for himself with you.”

“What sort of trouble is he in?” she wanted to know.

“I can’t tell you. It’s confidential. Let’s just say that he’d better keep his nose clean. Now. I need a few more things.” He brought out a list and handed it to her. She smiled and went off to fill the order for him.

He took the opportunity to have a last word with Tarleton.

“I hear you have a penchant for getting even with people who cross you,” John said. His eyes narrowed and began to glitter. “For the record, if you touch that girl, or if you even try to cause problems for her of any sort, you’ll have to deal with me. I don’t threaten people with lawsuits. I get even.” The way he said it, added to his even, unblinking glare, had backed down braver men than this middle-aged molester.

Tarleton tried to put on a brave front, but the man’s demeanor was unsettling. Taggert was younger than Tarleton and powerfully muscled for all his slimness. He didn’t look like a man who ever walked away from a fight.

“I wouldn’t touch her in a blind fit,” the older man said haughtily. “I just want to work out my notice and get the hell back to Billings, where people are more civilized.”

"Good idea," John replied. "Follow it."

He turned on his heel and went back to Sas

She looked even more nervous now. "Wha you say to him?" she asked uneasily, bec Tarleton looked at her as if he'd like her servec on a spit.

"Nothing of any consequence," he said eası and he gave her a tender smile. "Got my ord ready?"

"Most of it," she said, obviously trying to get he mind back to business. "But we don't carry any o this grass seed you want. It would be specia order." She leaned forward. "The hardware store can get it for you at a lower price, but I think we will be faster."

He grinned. "The price won't matter to my boss," he assured her. "But speed will. He's experimenting with all sorts of forage grasses. He's looking for better ways to increase weight without resorting to artificial means. He thinks the older grasses have more nutritional benefit than the hybrids being sowed today."

"He's likely right," she replied. "Organic methods are gaining in popularity. You wouldn't believe how many organic gardeners we have locally."

"That reminds me. I need some insecticidal soap for the beans we're planting."

She hesitated.

He cocked his head. His eyes twinkled. "You

/ant to tell me something, but you're not sure ou should."

She laughed. "I guess so. One of our organic gá ıeners gave up on it for beans. She says it worl nicely for tomatoes and cucumbers, but you neec something with a little more kick for beans and corn. She learned that the hard way." She grimaced. "So did I. I lost my first corn planting to corn borers and my beans to bean beetles. I was determined not to go the harsh pesticide route."

"Okay. Sell me something harsh, then," he chuckled.

She blushed faintly before she pulled a sack of powerful but environmentally safe insecticide off the shelf and put it on the counter.

Tarleton was watching the byplay with cold, angry eyes. So she liked that interfering cowboy, did she? It made him furious. He was certain that the new foreman of the Bradbury ranch had talked to someone about him and passed the information on to McGuire, who owned this feed store. The cowboy was arrogant for a man who worked for wages, even for a big outfit like the Callisters'. He was losing his job for the second time in six months and it would look bad on his record. His wife was already sick of the moving. She might leave him. It was a bad day for him when John Taggert walked into his store. He hoped the man fell in a well and drowned, he really did.

His small eyes lingered on Sassy's trim figure.

She really made him hot. She wasn't the sort to put up much of a fight, and that man Taggert couldn't watch her day and night. Tarleton smiled coldly to himself. If he was losing his job anyway, he didn't have much to lose. Might as well get something out of the experience. Something sweet.

Sassy went home worn-out at the end of the week. Tarleton had found more work than ever before for her to do, mostly involving physical labor. He was rearranging all the shelves with the heaviest items like chicken mash and hog feed and horse feed and dog food in twenty-five and fifty-pound bags. Sassy could press fifty pounds, but she was slight and not overly muscular. It was uncomfortable. She wished she could complain to someone, but if she did, it would only make things worse. Tarleton was getting even because he'd been fired. He watched her even more than he had before, and it was in a way that made her very uncomfortable.

Her mother was lying on the sofa watching television when Sassy got home. Little Selene was playing with some cut-outs. Her soft gray eyes lit up and she jumped up and ran to Sassy, to be picked up and kissed.

"How's my girl?" Sassy asked, kissing the soft little cheek.

"I been playing with Dora the Explorer, Sassy!" the little blond girl told her. "Pippa gave them to me at school!"

Pippa was the daughter of a teacher and her husband, a sweet child who always shared her playthings with Selene. It wasn't a local secret that Sassy could barely afford to dress the child out of the local thrift shop, much less buy her toys.

"That was sweet of her," Sassy said with genuine delight.

"She says I can keep these ones," the child added.

Sassy put her down. "Show them to me."

Her mother smiled wearily up at her. "Pippa's mother is a darling."

Sassy bent and kissed her mother's brow. "So is mine."

Mrs. Peale patted her cheek. "Bad day?" she added.

Sassy only smiled. She didn't trouble her parent with her daily woes. The older woman had enough worries of her own. The cancer was temporarily in remission, but the doctor had warned that it wouldn't last. Despite all the hype about new treatments and cures, cancer was a formidable adversary. Especially when the victim was Mrs. Peale's age.

"I've had worse," Sassy told her. "What about pancakes and bacon for supper?" she asked.

"Sassy, we had pancakes last night," Selene complained as she showed her cut-outs to the woman.

"I know, baby," Sassy said, bending to kiss her

gently. "We have what we can afford. It isn't much."

Selene grimaced. "I'm sorry. I like pancakes," she added apologetically.

"I wish we could have something better," Sassy said. "If there was a better-paying job going, you can bet I'd be applying for it."

Mrs. Peale looked sad. "I'd hoped we could send you to college. At least to a vocational school. Instead we've caused you to land in a dead-end job."

Sassy struck a pose. "I'll have you know I'm expecting a prince any day," she informed them. "He'll come riding up on a white horse with an enormous bouquet of orchids, brandishing a wedding ring."

"If ever a girl deserved one," Mrs. Peale said softly, "it's you, my baby."

Sassy grinned. "When I find him, we'll get you one of those super hospital beds with a dozen controls so you can sit up properly when you want to. And we'll get Selene the prettiest dresses and shoes in the world. And then, we'll buy a new television set, one that doesn't have green people," she added, wincing at the color on the old console TV.

Pipe dreams. But dreams were all she had. She looked at her companions, her family, and decided that she'd much rather have them than a lot of money. But a little money, she sighed mentally, certainly would help their situation. Prince Charming existed, sadly, only in fairy tales.

The architect had his plans ready for the big barn. John approved them and told the man to get to work. Within a few days, building materials started arriving, carried in by enormous trucks: lumber, steel, sand, concrete blocks, bricks, and mortar and other construction equipment. The project was worth several million dollars, and it created a stir locally, because it meant jobs for many people who were having to commute to Billings to get work. They piled onto the old Bradbury place to fill out job applications.

John grinned at the enthusiasm of the new workers. He'd started the job with misgivings, wondering if it was sane to expect to find dozens of laborers in such a small, economically depressed area. But he'd been pleasantly surprised. He had new men from surrounding counties lining up for available jobs, experienced workers at that. He began to be optimistic.

He was doing a lot of business with the local feed store, but his presence was required on site while the construction was in the early stages. He'd learned the hard way that it wasn't wise to leave someone in charge without making sure they understood what was required during every step.

He felt a little guilty that he hadn't been back to

check that Sassy hadn't had problems with Tarleton, who only had two days left before he was being replaced. The new manager, Buck Mannheim, was already in town, renting a room from a local widow while he familiarized himself with the business. Tarleton, he told John, wasn't making it easy for him to do that. The man was resentful, surly, and he was making Sassy do some incredibly hard and unnecessary tasks at the store. Buck would have put a stop to it, but he felt he had no real authority until Tartleton's two weeks were officially up. He didn't want them to get sued.

As if that weasel would dare sue them, John thought angrily. But he didn't feel right putting Buck in the line of fire. The older man had come up here as a favor to Gil to run the business, not to go toe-to-toe with a belligerent soon-to-be-ex-employee.

"I'll handle this," John told the older man. "I need to stop by the post office anyway and get some more stamps."

"I don't understand why any man would treat a child so brutally," Buck said. "She's such a nice girl."

"She's not a girl, Buck," John replied.

"She's just nineteen," Buck replied, smiling. "I have a granddaughter that age."

John felt uncomfortable. "She seems older."

"She's got some mileage on her. A lot of responsibility. She needs help. That child her mother adopted goes to school in pitiful clothes. I know that most of the money they have is spent for utilities." He shook his head. "Hell of a shame. Her mother's little check is all used up for medicine that she has to take to stay alive."

John felt guilty that he hadn't looked into that situation. He hadn't planned to get himself involved with his employees' problems, and Sassy wasn't technically even that, but it seemed there was nobody else in a position to help. He frowned. "You said Sassy's mother was divorced? Where's her husband? Couldn't he help? Even if Sassy's not young enough for child support, she's still his child. She shouldn't have to be the breadwinner."

"He ran off with a young woman. Just walked out the door and left. He's never so much as called or written in the years he's been gone, since the divorce," Buck said knowledgeably. "From what I hear, he was a good husband and father. He couldn't fight his infatuation for the waitress." He shrugged. "That's life."

"I hope the waitress hangs him out to dry," John muttered darkly. "Sassy should never have been landed with so much responsibility at her age."

"She handles it well, though," Buck said admiringly. "She's the nicest young woman I've met in a long time. She earns her paycheck."

"She shouldn't be having to press weights to do

that," John replied. "I got too wrapped up in my barn to keep an eye on her. I'll make up for it today."

"Good for you. She could use a friend."

John walked in and noticed immediately how quiet it was. The front of the store was deserted. It was midmorning and there were no customers. He scowled, wondering why Sassy wasn't at the counter.

He heard odd sounds coming from the tack room. He walked toward it until he heard a muffled scream. Then he ran.

The door was locked from the inside. John didn't need ESP to know why. He stood back, shot a hard kick with his heavy work boots right at the door handle, and the door almost splintered as it flew open.

Tarleton had backed Sassy into an aisle of cattle feed sacks. He had her in a tight embrace and he was trying his best to kiss her. His hands were on her body. She was fighting for her life, panting and struggling against the fat man's body.

"You sorry, son of a . . . !" John muttered as he caught the man by his collar and literally threw him off Sassy.

She was gasping for air. Her blouse was torn and her shoulders ached. The stupid man had probably meant to do a lot more than just kiss her, if he'd locked the door, but thanks to John he'd barely gotten to first base. She almost gagged at the memory of his fat, wet mouth on her lips. She dragged her hand over it.

"You okay?" John asked her curtly.

"Yes, thanks to you," she said heavily. She glared at the man behind him.

He turned back toward Tarleton, who was flushed at being caught red-handed. He backed away from the homicidal maniac who started toward him with an expression that could have stopped traffic.

"Don't you . . . touch me . . . !" Tarleton protested.

John caught him by the shirtfront, drew back his huge fist, and knocked the man backward out into the feed store. He went after him, blue eyes sparking like live electricity, his big fists clenched, his jaw set rigidly.

"What the . . . ?" came a shocked exclamation from the front of the store.

A man in a business suit was standing there, eyebrows arching.

"Mr. . . . McGuire!" Tarleton exclaimed as he sat up on the floor holding his jaw. "He attacked me! Call the police!"

John glanced at McGuire with blazing eyes. "There's a nineteen-year-old girl in the tack room with her shirt torn off. Do you need me to draw you a picture?" he demanded.

McGuire's gray eyes suddenly took on the same

sheen as John's. He moved forward with an odd, gliding step and stopped just in front of Tarleton. He whipped out his cell phone and pressed in a number.

"Get over here," he said into the receiver. "Tarleton just assaulted Sassy! That's right. No, I won't let him leave!" He hung up. "You should have cut your losses and gone back to Billings," he told the white-faced man on the floor, nursing his jaw. "Now, you're going to jail."

"She teased me into doing it!" Tarleton cried. "It's her fault."

John glanced at McGuire. "And I'm a green elf." He turned on his heel and went back to the tack room to see about Sassy.

She was crying, leaning against an expensive saddle, trying to pull the ripped bits of her blouse closed. Her ratty little faded bra was visible where it was torn. It was embarrassing for her to have John see it.

John stripped off the cotton shirt he was wearing over his black undershirt. He eased her hands away from her tattered blouse and guided her arms into the shirt, still warm from his body. He buttoned it up to the very top. Then he framed her wet face in his big hands and lifted it to his eyes. He winced. Her pretty little mouth was bruised. Her hair was mussed. Her eyes were red and swollen.

"Me and my damned barn," he muttered. "I'm sorry."

"For . . . what?" she sobbed. "It's not your fault."

"It is. I should have expected something like this."

The bell on the door jangled and heavy footsteps echoed on wood. There was conversation, punctuated by Tarleton's protests.

A tall, lean man in a police uniform and a cowboy hat knocked at the tack door and walked in. John turned, letting him see Sassy's condition.

The newcomer's thin mouth set in hard lines and his black eyes flashed fire. "You all right, Sassy?" he asked in a deep, bass voice.

"Yes, sir, Chief Graves," she said brokenly. "He assaulted me!" she accused, glaring at Tarleton. "He came up behind me while I was putting up stock and grabbed me. He kissed me and tore my blouse . . ." Her voice broke. "He tried to . . . to . . . !" She couldn't choke the word out.

Graves looked as formidable as John. "He won't ever touch you again. I promise. I need you to come down to my office when you feel a little better and give me a statement. Will you do that?"

"Yes, sir."

He glanced at John. "You hit him?" he asked, jerking his head toward the man still sitting on the floor outside the room.

"Damned straight I did," John returned belligerently. His blue eyes were still flashing with bad temper.

Chief Graves glanced at Sassy and winced.

The police chief turned and went back out into the other room. He caught Tarleton by his arm, jerked him to his feet, and handcuffed him while he read him his rights.

"You let me go!" Tarleton shouted. "I'm going back to Billings in two days. She lied! I never touched her that way! I just kissed her! She teased me! She set me up! She lured me into the back! And I want that damned cowboy arrested for assault! He hit me!"

Nobody was paying him the least bit of attention. In fact, the police chief looked as if he'd like to hit Tarleton himself. The would-be Romeo shut up.

"I'm never hiring anybody else as long as I live," McGuire told the police chief. "Not after this."

"Sometimes snakes don't look like snakes," Graves told him. "We all make mistakes. Come along, Mr. Tarleton. We've got a nice new jail cell for you to live in while we get ready to put you on trial."

"She's lying!" Tarleton raged, red-faced.

Sassy came out with John just behind her. The ordeal she'd endured was so evident that the men in the room grimaced at just the sight of her. Tarleton stopped shouting. He looked sick.

"Do you mind if I say something to him, Chief Graves?" Sassy asked in a hoarse tone.

"Not at all," the lawman replied.

She walked right up to Tarleton, with her green eyes glittering with fury, drew back her hand, and slapped him across the mouth as hard as she could. Then she turned on her heel and walked right back to the counter, picked up a sack of seed corn that she'd left there when the assault began, and went back to work.

The three men glanced from her to Tarleton. Their faces wore identical expressions.

"I'll get a good lawyer!" Tarleton said belligerently.

"You'll need one," John promised him, in a tone so full of menace that the man backed up a step.

"I'll sue you for assault!" he said from a safe distance.

"The corporation's attorneys will enjoy the exercise," John told him coolly. "One of them graduated from Harvard and spent ten years as a prosecutor specializing in sexual assault cases."

Tarleton looked sick.

Graves took him outside. John turned to McGuire.

The man in the suit rammed his hands into his pockets and grimaced. "I'll never be able to make that up to her," he said heavily.

"You might tell her that you recommended raising her salary," John replied.

"It's the least I can do," he agreed. "That new employee of yours—Buck Mannheim. He's sharp. I learned things I didn't know just from spending a half hour talking to him. He'll be an asset."

John nodded. "He retired too soon. Sixty-five is no great age these days." He glanced toward the back, where Sassy was moving things around. "She needs to see a doctor."

"Did Tarleton . . . ?" McGuire asked with real concern.

John shook his head. "But he would have. If I'd walked in just ten minutes later . . ." His face paled as he considered what would have happened. "Damn that man! And damn me! I should have realized he'd do something stupid to get even with her!"

"I should have realized, too," McGuire added. "Don't beat yourself to death. There's enough guilt to share. Dr. Bates is next to the post office. He has a clinic. He'll see her. He's been her family physician since she was a child."

"I'll take her right over there."

Sassy looked up when John approached her. She looked terrible, but she wasn't crying anymore. "Is he going to fire me?" she asked John.

"What in hell for? Almost getting raped?" he exclaimed. "Of course not. In fact, he's mentioned getting you a raise. But right now, he wants you to go to the doctor and get checked out."

"I'm okay," she protested. "And I have a lot of work to do."

"It can wait."

"I don't want to see Dr. Bates," she said.

He shrugged. "We're both pretty determined about this. I don't really think you'd like the way I deal with mutiny."

She stuck her hands on her slender hips. "Oh, yeah? Let's see how you deal with it."

He smiled gently. Before she could say another word, he picked her up very carefully in his arms and walked out the front door with her.

CHAPTER THREE

"YOU can't do this!" Sassy raged as he walked across the street with her, to the amusement of an early morning shopper in front of the small grocery store there.

"You won't go voluntarily," he said philosophically. He looked down at her and smiled gently. "You're very pretty."

She stopped arguing. "W . . . what?"

"Pretty," he repeated. "You've got grit, too." He chuckled. "I wish you'd half-closed that hand you hit Tarleton with, though." The smile faded. "That piece of work should be thrown into the county detention center wearing a sign telling what he tried to do. They'd pick him up in a shoebox."

Her small hands clung to his neck. "I didn't see it coming," she said, still in shock. "He pushed me into the tack room and locked the door. Before I could save myself, he pushed me back into the feed sacks and started kissing me and trying to get inside my blouse. I never thought I'd get away. I was fighting for all I was worth . . ." She swallowed hard. "Men are so strong. Even pudgy men like him."

"*I* should have seen it coming," he said, staring ahead with a set face. "A man like that doesn't go quietly. This could have been a worse tragedy than it already is."

"You saved me."

He looked down into her wide, green eyes. "Yes. I saved you."

She managed a wan smile. "Funny. I was just talking to Selene—my mother's little ward—about how Prince Charming would come and rescue me one day." She studied his handsome face. "You do look a little like a prince."

His eyebrow jerked. "I'm too tall. Princes are short and stubby, mostly."

"Not in movies."

"Ah, but that's not real life."

"I'll bet you don't know a single prince."

She'd have been amazed. He and his brother had rubbed elbows with crowned heads of Europe any number of times. But he couldn't admit that, of course.

"You could be right," he agreed easily.

He paused to open the door with one hand with Sassy propped on his knee. He walked into the doctor's waiting room with Sassy still in his arms and went up to the receptionist behind her glass panel. "We have something of an emergency," he said in a low tone. "She's been the victim of an assault."

"Sassy?" the receptionist, a girl Sassy had gone to school with, exclaimed. She took one look at the other girl's face and went running to open the door for John. "Bring her right in here. I'll get Dr. Bates!"

The doctor was a crusty old fellow, but he had a kind heart and it showed. He asked John to wait outside while he examined his patient. John stood in the hall, staring at anatomy charts that lined the painted concrete block wall. In no time the sliding door opened and he motioned John back into the cubicle.

"Except for some understandable emotional upset, and a few light bruises, she's not too hurt." The doctor glowered. "I would like to see her assailant spend a few months or, better yet, a few years, in jail, however."

"So would I," John told him, looking glittery and full of outrage. "In fact, I'm going to work on that."

The doctor nodded. "Good man." He turned to Sassy, who was quiet and pale now that her ordeal was over and reaction was starting to set in. "I'm going to inject you with a tranquilizer. I want you to go home and lie down for the rest of the day." He held up a hand when she protested. "Selene's in school and your mother will cope. It's not a choice, Sassy," he added as he leaned out of the cubicle and motioned to a nurse.

While he was giving the nurse orders, John stuck his hands in his jeans pockets and looked down at Sassy. She had grit and style, for a woman raised in the back of beyond. He admired her. She was pretty, too, although she didn't seem to realize it. The only real obstacle was her age. His face closed up as he faced the fact that she was years too young for him, even without their social separation. It was a pity. He'd been looking all his adult life for a woman he could like as well as desire. This sweet little firecracker was unique in his female acquaintances. He admired her.

His pale eyes narrowed on Sassy's petite form. She had a very sexy body. He loved those small, pert breasts under the cotton shirt. He thought how bruised they probably were from Tarleton's fingers and he wanted to hurt the man all over again. He knew she was untouched. Tarleton had stolen her first intimacy from her, soiled it, demeaned it. He wished he'd wiped the floor with the man before the police chief came.

Sassy saw his expression and felt uneasy. Did he think she was responsible for the attack? She winced. He didn't know her at all. Maybe he thought she had lead Tarleton on. Maybe he thought she'd deserved what happened to her.

She lowered her eyes in shame. The doctor came back in with a syringe, rolled up her sleeve, swiped her upper arm with alcohol on a cotton ball, and injected her. Sassy didn't even flinch. She rolled down her sleeve.

"Go home before that takes effect, or you'll be lying down in the road," the doctor chuckled. He glanced at John. "Can you . . . ?"

"Of course," John said. He smiled at Sassy, allaying her fears about his attitude. "Come on, sprout. I'll drive you."

"There's new stock that has to be put up in the store," she began to protest.

"It will still be waiting for you in the morning. If Buck needs help, I'll send some of my men into town to help him."

"But it's not your responsibility . . ."

"My boss has leased the feed store," he reminded her. "That makes it my responsibility."

"All right, then." She turned her head and smiled at the doctor. "Thanks."

He smiled back. "Don't you let this take over your life," he lectured her. "If you have any problems, you come back. I know a psychologist who works for the school system. She also takes private patients. I'll send you to her."

"I'll be okay."

John nodded at the doctor and followed Sassy out the door.

On the way home, Sassy sat beside him in the cab of the big pickup truck, fascinated by all the high-tech gadgets. "This is really nice," she remarked, smoothing over the leather dash. “I’ve never seen so many buttons and switches in a truck before.”

He smiled lazily, steering with his left hand while he toyed with a loaded key ring in one of the big cup holders. “We use computers for roundup and GPS to move cattle and men around.”

“Do you have a phone in here?” she asked, looking for one.

He indicated the second cup holder, where his cell phone was sitting. “I’ve got Bluetooth wiring in here,” he explained. “The phone works through the speaker system. It’s hands free. I can shorthand the call by saying the first or last name of the person I want to call. The phone does the rest. I get the Internet on it, and my e-mail as well.”

“Wow,” she said softly. “It’s like the *Starship Enterprise*, isn’t it?”

He could have told her that his brand-new Jaguar XF was more in that line, with controls that rose out of the console when the push-button ignition was activated, backup cameras, heated seats and steering wheel, and a supercharged V8 engine. But he wasn’t supposed to be able to afford that sort of luxury, so he kept his mouth shut.

“This must be a very expensive truck,” she murmured.

He grinned. “Just mid-range. Our bosses don’t skimp on tools,” he told her. “That includes working equipment for assistant feed store managers as well.”

She looked at him through green eyes that were becoming drowsy. “Are we getting a new assistant manager to go with Mr. Mannheim?” she asked.

“Sure. You,” he added, glancing at her warmly. “That goes with a rise in salary, by the way.”

Her breath caught. “Do you mean it?”

“Of course.”

“Wow,” she said softly, foreseeing better used appliances for the little house and some new clothes for Selene. “I can’t believe it!”

“You will.” He frowned. “Don’t fall over in your seat.”

She laughed breathily. “I think the shot’s taking effect.” She moved and grimaced, absently touching her small breasts. “A few bruises are coming out, too. He really was rough.”

His face hardened. “I hate knowing he manhandled you,” he said through his teeth. “I wish I’d come to the store sooner.”

“You saved me, just the same,” she replied. She smiled. “My hero.”

He chuckled. “Not me, lady,” he mused. “I’m just a working cowboy.”

“There’s nothing wrong with honest labor and hard work,” she told him. “I could never wrap my mind around some rich, fancy man with a string of women following him around. I like cowboys just fine.”

The words stung. He was living a lie, and he shouldn’t have started out with her on the wrong foot. She was an honest person. She'd never trust him again if she realized how he was fooling her. He should tell her who he really was. He glanced in her direction. She was asleep. Her head was resting against the glass, her chest softly pulsing as she breathed.

Well, there would be another time, he assured himself. She'd had enough shocks for one day.

He pulled up in her driveway, went around and lifted her out of the truck in his arms. He paused at the foot of the steps to look down at her sleeping face. He curled her close against his chest, loving her soft weight, loving the sweet face pressed against his shirt pocket. He carried her up the steps easily, knocked perfunctorily at the door, and opened it.

Her mother, Mrs. Peale, was sitting in a chair in her bathrobe, watching the news. She cried out when she saw her daughter.

"What happened to her?" she exclaimed, starting to rise.

"She's all right," he said at once. "The doctor sedated her. Can I put her down somewhere, and I'll explain."

"Yes. Her bedroom . . . is this way." She got to her feet, panting with the effort.

"Mrs. Peale, you just point the way and sit back down," he said gently. "You don't need to strain yourself."

Her kind face beamed in a smile. “You’re a nice young man. It’s the first door on the left. Her bedroom.”

“I’ll be right back.”

He carried Sassy into the bare little room and pulled back the worn blue chenille coverlet that was on the twin bed where she slept. Everything was spotless, if old. He lifted Sassy’s head onto the pillow, tugged off her boots, and drew the coverlet over her, patting it down at her waist.

She breathed regularly. His eyes went from her disheveled, wavy dark hair to the slight rise of her firm breasts under the shirt he’d loaned her, down her narrow waist and slender hips and long legs. She was attractive. But it was more than a physical attractiveness. She was like a warm fireplace on a cold day. He smiled at his own imagery, took one last look at her pretty, sleeping face, went out, and pulled the door gently closed behind him.

Mrs. Peale was watching for him, worried. “What happened to her?” she asked at once.

He sat down on the sofa next to her chair. “She’s had a rough day . . .”

“That Tarleton man!” Mrs. Peale exclaimed furiously. “It was him, wasn’t it?”

His eyebrows arched at her unexpected perception. “Yes,” he agreed slowly. “But how would you know . . . ?”

“He’s been creeping around her ever since McGuire hired him,” she said in her soft, raspy voice. She paused to get her breath. Her green eyes, so much like Sassy's, were sparking with temper. "She came home crying one day because he touched her in a way he shouldn't have, and she couldn't stop him. He thought it was funny."

John's usually placid face was drawn with anger as he listened.

Mrs. Peale noticed that, and the caring way he'd brought her daughter home. "Forgive me for being blunt, but, who are you?" she asked gently.

He smiled. "Sorry. I'm John . . . Taggert," he added, almost caught off guard enough to tell the truth. "My boss bought the old Bradbury place, and I'm his foreman."

"That place." She seemed surprised. "You know, it's haunted."

His eyebrows arched. "Excuse me?"

"I'm sorry. I shouldn't have said that . . . !" she began quickly.

"No. Please. I'd like to know," he said, reassuring her. "I collect folk tales."

She laughed breathily. "I guess it could be called that. You see, it began a long time ago when Hart Bradbury married his second cousin, Miss Blanche Henley. Her father hated the Bradburys and opposed the marriage, but Blanche ran away with Hart and got married to him anyway. Her father swore vengeance. One day, not long afterward, Hart came home from a long day gathering in strays, and found Blanche apparently in the arms of another man. He threw her out of his house and made her go back home to her father."

"Don't tell me," John interrupted with a smile. "Her father set her up."

"That's exactly what he did, with one of his men. Blanche was inconsolable. She sat in her room and cried. She did no cooking and no housework and she stopped going anywhere. Her father was surprised, because he thought she'd take up her old responsibilities with no hesitation. When she didn't, he was stuck with no help in the house and a daughter who embarrassed him in front of his friends. He told her to go back to her husband if he'd have her.

"So she did. But Hart met her at the door and told her he'd never live with her again. She'd gone from him to another man, or so he thought. Blanche gave up. She walked right out the side porch onto that bridge beside the old barn, and threw herself off the top. Hart heard her scream and ran after her, but she hit her head on a boulder when she went down, and her body washed up on the shore. Hart knew then that she was innocent. He sent word to her father that she'd killed herself. Her father went rushing over to Hart's place. Hart was waiting for him, with a double-barreled shotgun. He gave the old man one barrel and saved the other for himself." She grimaced. "It was almost ninety years ago, but nobody's forgotten."

"But they call the ranch the Bradbury place, don't they?" John asked, puzzled.

Mrs. Peale smiled. "Hart had three brothers. One of them took over the property. That was the great-uncle of the Bradbury you bought the ranch from."

"Talk about tragedies that stick in the mind," John mused. "I'm glad I'm not superstitious."

"How is it that you ended up bringing my daughter home?" she wondered aloud.

"I walked into the tack room in time to save her from Tarleton," he replied simply. "She didn't want to go to the doctor, so I carried her across the street and into his office." He sighed. "I suppose gossips will feed on that story for a week."

Mrs. Peale laughed. She had to stop suddenly, because her weak lungs wouldn't permit much of it. "Sassy is very stubborn."

He nodded. "I noticed." He smiled. "But she's got grit."

"Will she be all right?" she asked, worried.

"The doctor said that, apart from some bruises, she will. Of course there's the trauma of the attack itself."

"We'll deal with that . . . if we have to," the old woman said quietly. She bit her lower lip. "Do you know about me?" she asked suddenly.

"Yes, I do," he replied.

Her thin face was drawn. "Sassy has nobody. My husband ran off and left me with Sassy still in school. I took in Selene when her father died while he was working for us, just after Sassy's father left. We have no living family. When I'm gone," she added slowly, "she won't have anybody at all."

"She'll be all right," John assured her quietly. "We've promoted her to assistant manager of the feed store. It comes with a raise in salary. And if she ever needs help, she'll get it. I promise."

She turned her head like a bird watching him. "You have an honest face," she said after a minute. "Thank you, Mr. Taggert."

He smiled. "She's sweet."

"Sweet and unworldly," she said heavily. "This is a good place to raise children, but it doesn't give them much sense of modern society. She's a babe in the woods, in some ways."

"She'll be fine," he assured her. "Sassy may be naïve, but she has an excellent self-image and she's a strong woman. If you could have seen her swinging on Tarleton," he added on a chuckle, with admiration in his pale eyes.

"She hit him?" she exclaimed.

"She did," he replied. "I wish they'd given her five minutes alone with him. It might have cured him of ever wanting to force himself on another woman. Not," he added darkly, "that he's going to have the opportunity for a very long time. The police chief has him in jail pending arraignment. He'll be brought up on assault charges and, I assure you, he won't be running around town again."

"Mr. McGuire should never have hired him," she muttered.

"I can assure you that he knows that."

She bit her lip. "What if he gets a good lawyer and they turn him loose?"

"In that case," John chuckled, "we'll search and find enough evidence on crimes in his past to hang him out to dry. Whatever happens, he won't be a threat to Sassy ever again."

Mrs. Peale beamed. "Thank you for bringing her home."

"Do you have a telephone here?" he asked suddenly.

She hesitated. "Yes, of course."

He wondered at the hesitation, but not just then. "If you need anything, anything at all, you can call me." He pulled a pencil and pad out of his pocket, one he'd bought in town to list supplies, and wrote the ranch number on it. He handed it to Mrs. Peale. "Somebody will be around all the time."

"That's very kind of you," she said quietly.

"We help each other out back home," he told her. "That's what neighbors are for."

"Where is back home, Mr. Taggert?" she asked curiously.

"The Callisters we work for live at Medicine Ridge," he told her.

"Those people!" She caught her breath. "My goodness, everybody knows who they are. In fact, we had a man who used to work for them here in town."

John held his breath. "You did?"

"Of course, he moved on about a year ago," she added, and didn't see John relax. "He said they were the best bosses on earth and that he'd never have left if his wife hadn't insisted she had to be near her mother. Her mother was like me," she added sadly, "going downhill by the day. You can't blame a woman for feeling like that. I stayed with my own mother when she was dying." She looked up. "Are your parents still living?"

He smiled. "Yes, they are. I don't know them very well yet, but all of us are just beginning to get comfortable with each other."

"You were estranged?"

He nodded. "But not anymore. Can I do anything for you before I leave?"

"No, but thank you."

"I'll lock the door on my way out."

She smiled at him.

"I'll be out this way again," he said. "Tell Sassy she doesn't have to come in tomorrow unless she just wants to."

"She'll want to," Mrs. Peale said confidently. "In spite of that terrible man, she really likes her work."

"I like mine, too," John told her. He winked. "Good night."

"Good night, Mr. Taggert."

He drove back to the Bradbury place deep in thought. He wished he could make sure that

Tarleton didn't get out of jail anytime soon. He was still worried. The man was vindictive. He'd assaulted Sassy for reporting his behavior. God knew what he'd do to her if he managed to get out of that jail. He'd have to talk to Chief Graves and see if there was some way to get his bond set sky-high.

The work at the ranch was coming along quickly. The framework for the barn was already up. Wiring and plumbing were in the early stages. A crew was starting to remodel the house. John had one bedroom as a priority. He was sick of using a sleeping bag on the floor.

He phoned Gil that night. "How are things going at home?" he asked.

Gil chuckled. "Bess brought a snake to the dinner table. You've never seen women run so fast!"

"I'll bet Kasie didn't run," he mused.

"Kasie tickled it under the chin and told Bess it was the prettiest garter snake she'd ever seen."

"Your new wife is a delight," John murmured.

"And you can stop right there," Gil muttered. "She's my wife. Don't you forget that."

John burst out laughing. "You can't possibly still be jealous of her now!"

"I can, too."

"I could bring her truckloads of flowers and hands full of diamonds, and she'd still pick you,"

John pointed out. "Love trumps material possessions. I'm just her brother-in-law now."

"Well, okay," Gil said after a minute. "How are the improvements coming along?"

"Slowly," John sighed. "I'm still using a sleeping bag on the hard floor. I've given them orders to finish my bedroom first. Meanwhile, I'm getting the barn put up. Oh, and I've leased us a feed store."

There was a pause. "Should I ask why?"

"The manager tried to assault a young woman who's working for the store. He's in jail."

"And you leased the store because . . . ?"

John sighed. "The girl's mother is dying of lung cancer," he said heavily. "There's a young girl they took in when her father died . . . she's six. Sassy is the only one bringing in any money. I thought if she could be promoted to assistant manager, she might be able to pay her bills and buy a few new clothes for the little girl."

"Sassy, hmmm?"

John flushed at that knowing tone. "Listen, she's just a girl who works there."

"What does she look like?"

"She's slight. She has wavy, dark hair and green eyes and she's pretty when she smiles. When I pulled Tarleton off her, she walked up and slapped him as hard as she could. She's got grit."

"Tarleton would be the manager?"

"Yes," John said through his teeth. "The owner

of the store, McGuire, hired him long distance and moved him here with his wife. Tarleton's lost at least one job for sexual harassment."

"Then why the hell did McGuire hire him?"

"He didn't know about the charges—there was never a conviction. He said he was desperate. Nobody wanted to work in this outback town."

"So who are we going to get to replace him?"

"Buck Mannheim."

"Good choice," Gil said. "Buck was dying of boredom after he retired. The store will be a challenge for him."

"He's a good manager. Sassy likes him already, and she knows every piece of merchandise on the place and the ordering system like the back of her hand. She keeps the place stocked."

"Is she all right?"

"A little bruised," John said. "I took her to the doctor and then drove her home. She slept all the way there."

"She didn't fuss about having the big boss carting her around?" Gil asked amusedly.

"Well, she doesn't know that I am the big boss," John returned.

"She what?"

John scowled. "Why does she have to know who I am?"

"You'll get in trouble if you start playing with the truth."

"I'm not playing with it. I'm just sidestepping it

for a little while. I like having people take me at face value for a change. It's nice to be something more than a walking checkbook."

Gil cleared his throat. "Okay. It's your life. Let's just hope your decision doesn't come back to bite you down the line."

"It won't," John said confidently. "I mean, it isn't as if I'm planning anything permanent here. By the time I'm ready to come back to Medicine Ridge, it won't matter, anyway."

Gil changed the subject. But John wondered if there might not be some truth in what his big brother was saying. He hoped there wasn't. Surely it wasn't a bad thing to try to live a normal life for once. After all, he asked himself, how could it hurt?

CHAPTER FOUR

SASSY settled in as assistant manager of the feed store. Buck picked at her gently, teased her, and made her feel so much at home that it was like belonging to a family. During her second week back at work, she asked permission to bring Selene with her to work on the regular Saturday morning shift. Her mother had had a bad couple of days, she explained, and she wasn't well enough to watch Selene. Buck said it was all right.

But when John walked into the store and found a six-year-old child putting up stock, he wasn't pleased.

"This is a dangerous place for a kid," he told Sassy gently. "Even a bridle bit falling from the wall could injure her."

Sassy stopped and stared at him. "I hadn't thought about that."

"And there are the pesticides," he added. "Not that I think she'd put any in her mouth, but if she dropped one of those bags, it could fly up in her face." He frowned. "We had a little girl on the ranch back in Medicine Ridge who had to be transported to the emergency room when a bag of garden insecticide tore and she inhaled some of it."

"Oh, dear," Sassy said, worried.

"I don't mind her being here," John assured her. "But find her something to do at the counter. Don't let her wander around. Okay?"

She cocked her head at him. "You know a lot about kids."

He smiled. "I have nieces about Selene's age," he told her. "They can be a handful."

"You love them."

"Indeed I do," he replied, his eyes following Selene as she climbed up into a chair at the counter, wearing old but clean jeans and a T-shirt. "I've missed out on a family," he added quietly. "I never seemed to have time to slow down and think about permanent things."

"Why not?" she asked curiously.

His pale eyes searched hers quietly. "Pressure of

work, I suppose," he said vaguely. "I wanted to make my mark in the world. Ambition and family life don't exactly mesh."

"Oh, I get it," she said, and smiled up at him. "You wanted to be something more than just a working cowboy."

His eyebrow jerked. "Something like that," he lied. The mark he meant was to have, with his brother, a purebred breeding herd that was known all over the world—a true benchmark of beef production that had its roots in Montana. The Callisters had attained that reputation, but John had sacrificed for it, spending his life on the move, going from one cattle show to another with the ranch's prize animals. The more awards their breeding bulls won, the more they could charge for their progeny.

"You're a foreman now," she said. "Could you get higher up than that?"

"Sure," he said, warming to the subject. He grinned. "We have several foremen, who handle everything from grain production to cattle production to AI," he added. "Above that, there's ranch management."

Her eyebrows drew together. "AI?" she queried. "What's that?"

If she'd been older and more sophisticated, he might have teased her with the answer. As it was, he took the question at face value. "It's artificial breeding," he said gently. "We hire a man who comes out with the product and inseminates our cows and heifers."

She looked uncomfortable. "Oh."

He smiled. "It's part of ranch protocol," he said, his tone soft. "The old-fashioned way is hit or miss. In these hard times, we have to have a more reliable way of insuring progeny."

She smiled back shyly. "Thanks for not explaining it in a crude way," she said. "We had a rancher come in here a month ago who wanted a diaper for his female dog, who was in heat." She flushed a little. "He thought it was funny when I got uncomfortable at the way he talked about it."

His thumb hooked into his belt as he studied her. The comment made him want to find the rancher and have a long talk with him. "That sort of thing isn't tolerated on our spread," he said shortly. "We even have dress requirements for men and women. There's no sexual harassment, even in language."

She looked fascinated. "Really?"

"Really." He searched her eyes. "Sassy, you don't have to put up with any man talking to you in a way that embarrasses you. If a customer uses crude language, you go get Buck. If you can't find him, you call me."

"I never thought . . . I mean, it seemed to go with the job," she stammered. "Mr. Tarleton was worse than some of the customers. He used to try to guess the size of my . . . of my . . . well—" she shrugged, averting her eyes "—you know."

"Sadly, I do," he replied tersely. "Listen, you have to start standing up for yourself more. I know you're young, but you don't have to take being talked down to by men. Not in this job."

She rubbed an elbow and looked up at him like a curious little cat. "I was going to quit," she recalled, and laughed a little nervously. "I'd already talked to Mama about it. I thought even if I had to drive to Billings and back every day, I'd do it." She grimaced. "That was just before gas hit over four dollars a gallon." She sighed. "You'd have to be a millionaire to make that drive daily, now."

"I know," he said with heartfelt emotion. He and Gil had started giving their personnel a gas ration allowance in addition to their wages. "Which reminds me," he added with a smile, "we're adding gas mileage to the checks now. You won't have to worry about going bankrupt at the pump."

"That's so nice of you!"

He pursed his lips. "Of course. I am nice. It's one of my more sterling qualities. I mean, along with being debonair, a great conversationalist, and good at poker." He watched her reaction, smiling wickedly when she didn't quite get it. "Did I mention that dogs love me, too?"

She did get it then, and laughed shyly. "You're joking."

"Trying to."

She grinned at him. It made her green eyes light

up, her face radiant. "You must have a lot of responsibility, considering how much work they're doing out at your ranch."

"Yes, I do," he admitted. "Most of it involves organization."

"That sounds very stressful," she replied, frowning. "I mean, a big ranch would have an awful lot of people to organize. I would think that you'd have almost no free time at all."

He didn't have much free time. But he couldn't tell her why. Actually the little bit of time he'd already spent here, even working, was something like a holiday, considering the load he carried when he was at home. He and Gil between them were overworked. They delegated responsibility where they could, but some decisions could only be made by the boss. "Well, it's still sort of a goal of mine," he hedged. "A man has to have a little ambition to be interesting." He studied her with pursed lips. "What sort of job goals do you have?"

She blinked, thinking. "I don't have any, really. I mean, I want to take care of Mama as long as I can. And I want to raise Selene and make sure she has a good education, and to save enough to help her go to college."

He frowned. Her goals were peripheral. They involved helping other people, not in advancing herself. He'd never considered the future welfare of anyone except himself—well, himself and Gil and the girls and, now, Kasie. But Sassy was very young to be so generous, even in her thoughts.

Young. She was nineteen. His frown deepened as he studied her youthful, faintly flushed little face. He found her very attractive. She had a big heart, a nice smile, a pretty figure, and she was smart, in a common-sense sort of way. But that age hit him right in the gut every time he considered her part in his life. He didn't dare become involved with her.

"What's wrong?" she asked perceptively.

He shifted from one big, booted foot to the other. "I just had a stray thought," he told her. He glanced at Selene. "You've got a lot of responsibilities for a woman your age," he added quietly.

She laughed softly. "Don't I know it!"

His eyes narrowed. "I guess it cramps your social life. With men, I mean," he added, hating himself because he was curious about the men in her life.

She laughed. "There are only a couple of men around town who don't have wives or girlfriends, and I turn them off. One of them came right out and said I had too much baggage, even for a date."

His eyebrows arched. "And what did you say to that?"

"That I loved my mother and Selene and any man who got interested in me would have to take them on as well. That didn't go over big," she added with twinkling eyes. "So I've decided that I'm going to be like the Lone Ranger."

He blinked. "Masked and mysterious?"

"No!" she chuckled. "I mean, just me. Well, just me and my so-called dependents." She glanced toward Selene, who was quietly matching up seed packages from a box that had just arrived. Her eyes softened. "She's very smart. I can never sort things the way she can. She's patient and quiet, she never makes a fuss. I think she might grow up to be a scientist. She already has that sort of introspective personality, and she's careful in what she does."

"She thinks before she acts," he translated.

"Exactly. I tend to go rushing in without thinking about the consequences," she added with a laugh. "Not Selene. She's more analytical."

"Being impulsive isn't necessarily a bad thing," he remarked.

"It can be," she said. "But I'm working on that. Maybe in a few years, I'll learn to look before I leap." She glanced up at him. "How are things going out at the Bradbury place?"

"We've got the barn well underway already," he said. "The framework's done. Now we're up to our ears in roofers and plumbers and electricians."

"We only have a couple of each of those here in town," she pointed out, "and they're generally booked a week or two ahead except for emergencies."

He smiled. "We had to import some construction people from Billings," he told her. "It's a big job. Simultaneously, they're trying to make improvements to the house and plan a stable. We've got fencing to replace, wells to bore, agricultural equipment to buy . . . it's a monumental job."

"Your boss," she said slowly, "must be filthy rich, if he can afford to do all that right now when we've got gas prices through the roof!"

"He is," he confided. "But the ranch will be self-sufficient when we're through. We're using solar panels and windmills for part of our power generation."

"We had a city lawyer buy land here about six years ago," she recalled. "He put in solar panels to heat his house and all sorts of fancy, energy-saving devices." She winced. "Poor guy."

"Poor guy?" he prompted when she didn't continue.

"He saw all these nature specials and thought grizzly bears were cute and cuddly," she said. "One came up into his backyard and he went out with a bag full of bread to feed to it."

"Oh, boy," he said slowly.

She nodded. "The bear ate all the bread and when he ran out, it started eating him. He did manage to get away finally by playing dead, but he lost the use of an arm and one eye." She shook her head. "He was a sad sight."

"Don't tell me," he said. "He was from back East."

She nodded. "Some big city. He'd never seen a real bear before, except in zoos and nature specials. He saw an old documentary on this guy who lived with bears and he thought anybody could make friends with them."

"Reminds me of a story I heard about a lady from D.C. who moved to Arizona. She saw a rattlesnake crawling across the road, so the story goes, and thought it was fascinating. She got out of her car and walked over to pet it."

"What happened to her?"

"An uncountable number of shots of antivenin," he said, "and two weeks in the hospital."

"Ouch."

"You know all those warning labels they have on food these days? They ought to put warning labels on animals." He held both hands up, as if holding a sign. "Warning: Most wild reptiles are not cute and cuddly and they will bite and can kill you. Or, Grizzly bears will eat bread, fruit, and some people."

She laughed at his expression. "I ran from a grizzly bear once and managed to get away."

"Fast, are you?"

"He was old and slow, and I was close to town. But I had great incentive," she agreed.

"I've never had to outrun anything," he recalled. "I did once pet a moose who came up to serenade one of our milk cows. He was friendly."

"Isn't that unusual?"

"It is. Most wild animals that will let you close enough to pet them are rabid. But this moose wasn't sick. He just had no fear of humans. I think maybe he was raised as a pet by people who were smart enough not to tell anybody."

"Because . . . ?" she prompted.

"Well, it's against the law to make a pet of a wild animal in most places in the country," he explained. He smiled. "That moose loved corn."

"What happened to him?"

"He started charging other cattle to keep his favorite cow to himself, so we had to move him up farther into the mountains. He hasn't come back so far."

She grinned. "What if he does? Will you let him stay?"

He pursed his lips. "Sure! I plan to spray-paint him red, cut off his antlers, and tell people he's a French bull."

She burst out laughing at the absurd comment.

Selene came running up with a pad and pencil. " 'Scuse me," she said politely to John. She turned to her sister. "There's a man on the telephone who wants you to order something for him."

Sassy chuckled. "I'll go right now and take it down. Selene, this is John Taggert. He's a ranch foreman."

Selene looked up at him and grinned. She was missing one front tooth, but she was cute. "When I grow up, I'm going to be a fighter pilot!"

His eyebrows arched. "You are?"

"Yup! This lady came by to see my mama. She's

a nurse. Her daughter was a fighter pilot and now she flies big airplanes overseas!"

"Some role model," John remarked to Sassy, awed.

She laughed. "It's a brave new world."

"It is." He went down on one knee in front of Selene, so that her eyes could look into his. "And what sort of plane would you like to fly?" he teased, not taking her seriously.

She put a small hand on his broad shoulder. Her blue eyes were very wide and intent. "I like those F-22 Raptors," she said breathlessly. "Did you know they can actually stand still in the sky?"

He was fascinated. He wasn't sure he even knew what sort of military airplane that was. His breath exhaled. "No," he confessed. "I didn't."

"There was this program on TV about how they're built. And they were in a new movie about robots that come to our planet and pretend to be cars. I think Raptors are just beautiful," she said with a dreamy expression.

"I hope you get to fly one," he told her.

She smiled. "I got to grow up, first, though," she told him. She gasped. "Sassy!" she exclaimed. "That man's still on the phone!"

Sassy made a face. "I'm going, I'm going!"

"You coming back to see us again?" Selene asked John when he stood up.

He chuckled. "Thought I might."

“Okay!” She grinned and ran back to the counter, where Sassy was just picking up the phone.

John went to find Buck. It was a new world, indeed.

Tarleton was taken before the circuit judge for his arraignment and formally charged with the assault on Sassy. He pleaded not guilty. He had a city lawyer who gave the local district attorney a haughty glance and requested that his client, who was blameless, be let out on his own recognizance in lieu of bail. The prosecutor argued that Tarleton was a flight risk.

The judge, after reviewing the charges, did agree to set bail. But he set it at fifty thousand dollars, drawing furious protests from the attorney and his client. With no ability to raise such an amount, even using a bail bondsman, Tarleton would have to wait it out in the county detention facility. It wasn’t a prospect he viewed with pleasure.

Sassy heard about it and felt guilty. Mr. Tarleton, for all his flaws, had a wife who was surely not guilty of anything more than bad judgment in her choice of a husband. It seemed unfair that she would have to suffer along with the defendant.

She said so, to John, when he turned up at the store the end of the next week.

“His poor wife,” she sighed. “It’s so unkind to make her go through it with him.”

“Would you rather let him walk?” he asked quietly. "Set him free, so that he could do it to another young woman—perhaps with more tragic results?"

She flushed. "No. Of course not."

He reached out and touched her cheek with the tips of his fingers. "You have a big heart, Sassy," he said, his voice very deep and soft. "Plenty of other people don't, and they will use your own compassion against you."

She looked up curiously, tingling and breathless from just the faint contact of his fingers with her skin. "I guess some people are like that," she conceded. "But most people are kind and don't want to hurt others."

He laughed coldly. "Do you think so?"

His expression was saying things that she could read quite accurately. "Somebody hurt *you,*" she guessed. Her eyes held his. They had an odd, blank look in them. "A woman. It was a long time ago. You never talk about it. But you hold it inside, deep inside, and use it to keep the world at a distance."

He scowled. "You don't know me," he said, defensive.

"I shouldn't," she agreed. Her green eyes seemed darker, more piercing. "But I do."

"Don't tell me," he murmured with faint sarcasm, "you can read minds."

She shook her head. "I can read wrinkles."

"Excuse me?"

"Your frown lines are deeper than your smile

lines," she told him, not wanting to confess that her family had the "second sight," in case he thought she was peculiar. "It's a public smile. You leave it at the front door when you go home."

His eyes narrowed on her face. He didn't speak. She was incredibly perceptive for a woman her age.

She drew in a long breath. "Go ahead, say it. I need to mind my own business. I do try to, but it bothers me to see other people so unhappy."

"I am not unhappy," he said belligerently. "I'm very happy!"

"If you say so."

He glowered at her. "Just because a woman threw me over, I'm not damaged goods."

"How did she throw you over?"

He hadn't talked about it for years, not even to Gil. In one sense he resented this young woman, this stranger, prying into his life. In another, it made him want to talk about it, to stop the festering wound of it from growing even larger inside him.

"She got engaged to me while she was living with a man down in Colorado."

She didn't speak. She just watched him, like a curious little cat, waiting.

He grimaced. "I was so crazy about her that I never suspected a thing. She'd go away for weekends with her girlfriend and I'd watch movies and do book work at home while she was away. One weekend I had nothing to do, so I drove over to Red Lodge, where she'd said she was checked into a motel so that she could go fly-fishing with her girlfriend." He sighed. "Red Lodge isn't so big that you can't find people in it, and it does a big business in tourism. Turned out, her friend was male, filthy rich, and they had a room together. She had the most surprised look on her face when they came downstairs and found me sitting in the lobby."

"What did she say?" she asked.

"Nothing. Not one thing. She bit her lip and pretended that she didn't know the man. He was furious, and I felt like a fool. I went back home. She called and tried to talk to me, but I hung up on her. Some things don't take a lot of explaining."

He didn't add that he'd also hired a private detective, much too late, to find out what he could about the woman. It hadn't been the first time she'd kept a string of wealthy admirers, and she'd taken one man for a quarter of a million dollars before he found her out. She'd been after John's money, all along; not himself. He wasn't as forthcoming as the millionaire she'd gone fly-fishing with, so she'd been working on the millionaire while she left John simmering on a back burner. As a result, she'd lost both men, which did serve her right. But the experience had made him bitter and suspicious of all women. He still thought they only wanted him for his money.

"The other guy, was he rich?" Sassy asked.

John's lips made a thin line. "Filthy rich."

She touched the front of his shirt with a shy, hesitant little hand. "I'm sorry about that," she told him. "But in a way, you're lucky that you aren't rich," she added.

"Why?"

"Well, you never have to worry if women like you for yourself or your wallet," she said innocently.

"There isn't much to like," he said absently, concentrating on the way she was touching him. She didn't even seem to be aware of it, but his body was rippling inside with the pleasure it gave him.

"You're kidding, right?" she asked. Her eyes laughed up into his. "You're very handsome. You stand up for people who can't take care of themselves. You like children. And dogs like you," she added mischievously, recalling one of his earlier quips. "Besides that, you must like animals, since you work around cattle."

While she was talking, the hand on his chest had been joined by her other one, and they were flat on the broad, hard muscles, idly caressing. His body was beginning to respond to her touch in a profound way. His blue eyes became glittery with suppressed desire.

He caught her hands abruptly and moved them. "Don't do that," he said curtly, without thinking how it was going to affect her. He was in danger of losing control of himself. He wanted to reach for her, slam her against him all the way up and down, and kiss that pretty mouth until he made it swell and moan under his lips.

She jerked back, appalled at her own boldness. "I'm sorry," she said at once, flushing. "I really am. I'm not used to men. I mean, I've never done that . . . excuse me!"

She turned and all but ran back down the aisle to the counter. When she got there, she jerked up the phone and called a customer to tell him his order was in. She'd already phoned him, and he hadn't answered, so she called again. It gave her something to do, so that John thought she was getting busy.

He muttered under his breath. Now he'd done it. He hadn't meant to make her feel brassy with that comment, but she was starting to get to him. He wanted her. She had warmth and compassion and an exciting little body, and she was getting under his skin. He needed a break.

He turned on his heel and walked out of the store. He should have gone back and apologized for being so abrupt, but he knew he'd never be able to explain himself without telling her the truth. He couldn't do that. She was years too young for him. He had to get out of town for a while.

He left Bradbury's former ranch foreman, Carl Baker, in charge of the place while he packed and went home to Medicine Ridge for the weekend.

It was a warm, happy homecoming. His big

brother, Gil, met him at the door with a bear hug.

"Come on in," he said, chuckling. "We've missed you."

"Uncle John!"

Bess and Jenny, Gil's daughters by his first wife, came running down the hall to be picked up and cuddled and kissed.

"Oh, Uncle John, we missed you so much!" Bess, the eldest, cried, hugging him tightly around the neck.

"Yes, we did," Jenny seconded, kissing his bronzed cheek. "You can't stay away so long!"

"Did you bring us a present?" Bess asked.

He grinned. "Don't I always?" he laughed. "In the bag, next to my suitcase," he said, putting them down.

They ran to the bag, found the wrapped presents and literally tore the ribbons off to delve inside. There were two stuffed animals with bar codes that led children to Web sites where they could dress their pets and have adventures with them online in a safe environment.

"Web puppies!" Bess exclaimed, clutching a black Labrador.

Jenny had a Collie. She cuddled it close. "We seen these on TV!"

"Can we use the computer, Daddy?" Bess pleaded. "Please?"

"Use the computer?" Kasie, Gil's new wife, asked, grinning. "What are you babies up to, now?" she added, pausing to hug John before she pressed against Gil's side with warm affection.

"It's a Web puppy, Kasie!" Bess exclaimed, showing hers. "Uncle John bought them for us."

"I got a Collie, just like Lassie," Jenny beamed.

"We got to use the computer," Bess insisted.

Kasie chuckled. "I'll go start it up, then. Come on, babies. You staying for a while?" she asked John.

"For the weekend," John replied, smiling at the girls. "I needed a break."

"I guess you did," Gil replied. "You've taken on a big task up there. Sure you don't need more help? We could spare Green."

"I'm doing fine. Just a little complication."

Kasie led the girls off into Gil's office, where the computer lived. When they were out of earshot, Gil turned to John.

"What sort of complication?" he asked his younger brother.

John sighed. "There's a girl."

Gil's pale eyes sparkled. "It's about time."

John shook his head. "You don't understand. She's nineteen."

Gil only smiled. "Kasie was twenty-one. Barely. And I'm older than you are. Age doesn't have a lot to do with it."

John felt something of a load lift from his heart. "She's unworldly."

Gil chuckled. "Even better. Come have coffee and pie and tell me all about it!"

CHAPTER FIVE

SASSY put on a cheerful face for the rest of the day, pretending for all she was worth that having John Taggert push her away didn't bother her at all. It was devastating, though. She was shy with most men, but John had drawn her out of her shell and made her feel feminine and charming. Then she'd gone all googly over him and edged closer as if she couldn't wait to have him put his arms around her and kiss her. Even the memory of her behavior made her blush. She'd never been so forward with anyone.

Of course, she knew she wasn't pretty or desirable. He was a good deal older than she was, too, and probably liked beautiful and sophisticated women who knew their way around. He might not be a ranch boss, but he drove a nice truck and obviously made a good salary. In addition to all that, he was very handsome and charming. He'd be a woman magnet in any big city.

He'd saved her from Bill Tarleton, gotten her a raise and a promotion, and generally been kinder to her than she deserved. He probably had the shock of his life when she moved close to him as if she had the right, as if he belonged to her. The shame of it wore on her until she was pale and almost in tears when she left the shop that afternoon.

"Something bothering you, Sassy?" Buck Mannheim asked as they were closing up.

She glanced at him and forced a smile. "No, sir. Nothing at all. It's just been a long day."

"It's that Tarleton thing, isn't it?" he asked quietly. "You're upset that you'll have to testify."

She was glad to have an excuse for the way she looked. The assault did wear on her, but it was John Taggert's behavior, not her former boss's, that had her upset. "I guess it is a little worrying," she confessed.

He sighed. "Sassy, it's a sad fact of life that there are men like him in the world. But if you don't testify, he could get away with it. The reason you had trouble with him is that some other poor girl didn't want to have to face him in front of a jury. She let him walk. If he'd been convicted of sexual harassment, instead of just charged with it, he'd probably be in jail now. It might have stopped him from coming on to you."

She had to agree. "I suppose that's true. It's just . . . well, you know, Mr. Mannheim, some men think a woman leads them on if she just looks at them."

"I know. But that isn't the case here. John . . . Taggert—" he caught himself in the nick of time from letting John's real surname out "—will certainly testify to what he saw. He'll be there to back you up."

Which didn't make her feel any better, because

John would probably think she worked at leading men on, considering how he'd had to push her away from him for being forward. She couldn't say that to Mr. Mannheim. It was too embarrassing.

"You just go on home, have a nice dinner, and stop worrying," he said with a smile. "Everything is going to be all right."

She let out a breath and smiled. "You remind me of my grandfather. He always used to tell me that things worked out, if we just sat back and gave them a chance. He was the most patient person I ever knew."

"I'm not patient." Buck chuckled. "But I do agree with your grandfather. Time heals."

"Don't I wish," she mused. "Good night, Mr. Mannheim. See you in the morning."

"I'll be here."

She got into the battered old truck her grandfather had willed her on his death, and drove home with black smoke pouring out behind her. The vehicle was an embarrassment, but it was all she had. Just putting gas in it and keeping the engine from blowing up was exorbitant. She was grateful for the gas allowance that she'd gotten with her promotion. It would help financially.

She parked at the side of the rickety old house and studied it for a minute before she walked up onto the porch. It needed so much repair. The roof leaked, there was a missing board on the porch, the steps were starting to sag, at least two windows were rotting out . . . the list went on and on. She recalled what John had said about the improvements that were being made on the Bradbury place, and it wasn't in nearly as bad a shape as this place. She despaired about what she was going to do when winter came. Last winter, she'd barely been able to afford to fill one third of the propane tank they used to heat the house. There were small space heaters in both bedrooms and a stove with a blower in the living room. They'd had to ration carefully, so they'd used a lot of quilts during the coldest months, and tried their best to save on fuel costs. It looked as though this year the fuel price would be twice as much.

She didn't dare think about the obstacles that lay ahead, especially her mother's worsening health. If the doctor prescribed more medicine, they'd be over their heads in no time. She already owed the local pharmacy half her next week's paycheck, because she'd had to supplement the cost of her mother's extra pills.

Well, she had to stop thinking about that, she decided. People were more important than money. It was just that she was the only person making any money. Now she was going to be involved in a court case, and it was just possible that John's boss might hear about it and not want such a scandalous person working in his store. Worse, John might tell him about how forward she'd been in the feed store today. She couldn't forget how angry he'd been when he walked out.

Just as she started up the steps, the sky opened up and it began to rain buckets. There was no time to lose. There were three big holes in the ceiling. One was right over the television set. She couldn't afford to replace the enormous console television, which was her mother's only source of pleasure. It was almost twenty years old, and the color wasn't good, but it had lasted them since Sassy was a baby.

"Hi!" she called on her way down the hall.

"It's raining, dear!" her mother called from the bedroom.

"I know! I'm on it!"

She made a dash for the little plastic tub under the sink, ran into the living room, and made it just in the nick of time to prevent drips from overwhelming the TV set. It was too big and heavy to move by herself. Her mother couldn't do any lifting at all, and Selene was too small. Sassy couldn't budge it, so the only alternative was to protect it. She put the tub on the flat top and breathed a sigh of relief.

"Don't forget the leak in the kitchen!" Mrs. Peale called again. Her voice was very hoarse and thin.

Sassy grimaced. She sounded as if she was getting a bad case of bronchitis, and she wondered how she'd ever get her mother willingly loaded into the truck if she had to take her to town to Dr.

Bates. Maybe the dear old soul would make a house call, if he had to. He was a good man. He knew how stubborn Sassy's mother was, too.

She finished protecting the house with all sorts of buckets and pots. The drips on metal and plastic made a sort of soothing rhythm.

She peeked into her mother's bedroom. "Bad day?" she asked gently.

Her mother, pale and listless, nodded. "Hurts to cough."

Sassy felt even worse. "I'll call Dr. Bates . . ."

"No!" Her mother paused to cough again. "I've got antibiotics, Sassy, and I've used my breathing machine today already," she said gently. "I just need some cough syrup. It's on the kitchen counter." She managed a smile. "Try not to worry so much, darling," she coaxed. "Life just happens. We can't stop it."

Sassy bit her lower lip and nodded as tears threatened.

"Now, now." Mrs. Peale held out her thin arms. Sassy ran to the bed and into them, careful not to press on her mother's frail chest. She cried and cried.

"I'm not going to die yet," Mrs. Peale promised. "I have to see Selene through high school first!"

It was a standing joke. Usually they both laughed, but Sassy had been through the mill for the past week. Her life was growing more complicated by the hour.

"We had a visitor today," her mother said. "Guess who it was?"

Sassy wiped at her eyes and sat up, smiling through the tears. "Who?"

"Remember Brad Danner's son Caleb, that you had a crush on when you were fifteen?" she teased.

Memory produced a vague portrait of a tall, lanky boy with black eyes and black hair who'd never seemed to notice her at all. "Yes."

"He came by to see you," Mrs. Peale told her. "He's been in the Army, serving overseas. He stopped by to visit and wanted to say hello to you." She grinned. "I told him to come to supper."

Sassy caught her breath. "Supper?" She sat very still. "But we've only got stew, and just barely enough for us," she began.

Mrs. Peale chuckled hoarsely. "He said we needed some take-out, so he's bringing a bucket of chicken with biscuits and honey and cottage fries all the way from Billings. We can heat it back up in the oven if it's cold when he gets here."

"Real chicken?" Sassy asked, her eyes betraying her hunger for protein. Mostly the Peales ate stews and casseroles, with very little meat because it was so expensive. "And biscuits with honey?"

"I guess I looked like I was starving," Mrs. Peale said wistfully. "I didn't have the heart to refuse. He was so persuasive." She smiled sheepishly.

"You wicked woman," Sassy teased. "What did you do?"

"Well, I was very hungry. He was talking about what he'd gotten himself and his aunt for supper last night, and I did mention that I'd forgotten what a chicken tasted like. He volunteered to come to dinner and bring it with him. What could I say?"

Sassy bent and hugged her mother warmly. "At least you'll get one good meal this week," she mused. "So will Selene." She sat up, frowning. "Where is Selene?"

"She's in her room, doing homework," Mrs. Peale replied. "She studies so hard. We have to find a way to let her go to college if she wants to."

"We'll work it out," Sassy promised. "Her grades will probably be so high that she'll get scholarships all over the place. She's a good student."

"Just like you were."

"I goofed off more than Selene does."

"You should put on a nice pair of jeans and a clean shirt," she told her daughter. "You can borrow some of my makeup. Caleb is a handsome young man, and he isn't going with anybody."

"You didn't ask?" Sassy burst out, horrified.

"I asked in a very polite way."

"Mother!"

"You should never turn down a prospective suitor," she chuckled. The smile faded. "I know you like Mr. Taggert, Sassy, but there's something about him . . ."

Her heart sank. Her mother was oddly accurate

with her "feelings." "You don't think he's a criminal or something?"

"Silly girl. Of course not. I just mean that he seems out of place here," Mrs. Peale continued. "He's intelligent and sophisticated, and he doesn't act like the cowboys who work around here, haven't you noticed? He's the sort of man who would look at home in elegant surroundings. He's immaculate and educated."

"He told me that he wanted to be a ranch manager one day," Sassy confided. "He probably works at building the right image, to impress people."

"That could be. But I think there's more to him than shows."

"You and your intuition," Sassy chided.

"You have it, too," the older woman reminded her. "It's that old Scotch-Irish second sight. My grandmother had it as well. She could see far ahead." She frowned. "She made a prediction that never made sense. It still doesn't."

"What sort?"

"She said I would be poor, but my daughter would live like royalty." She laughed. "I'm sorry, darling, but that doesn't seem likely."

"Everyone's entitled to a few misses," Sassy agreed.

"Anyway, go dress up. I told Caleb that we eat at six."

Sassy grinned at her. "I'll dress up, but it won't

help. I'll still look like me, not some beauty queen."

"Looks fade. Character doesn't," her mother reminded her.

She sighed. "You don't find many young men in search of women with character."

"This may be the first. Hurry!"

Caleb was rugged-looking, tall and muscular and very polite. He smiled at Sassy and his dark eyes were intent on her face while he sat at the table with the two women and the little girl. He was serving in an Army unit in Afghanistan, where he was a corporal, he told them. He was a communications specialist, although he was good at fixing motors as well. The Army hadn't needed a mechanic when he enlisted, but they did need communications people, so he'd trained for that.

"Is it very bad over there, where you were?" Mrs. Peale asked, having struggled to the table with Caleb's help over Sassy's objections.

"Yes, it has been," Caleb said. "But we're making progress."

"Do you have to shoot people?" Selene asked.

"Selene!" Sassy exclaimed.

Caleb chuckled. "We try very hard not to," he told her. "But sometimes the warlords shoot at us. We're stationed high up in the mountains, where terrorists like to camp. We come under fire from time to time."

"It must be frightening," Sassy said.

"It is," Caleb said honestly. "But we do the jobs we're given, and try not to think about the danger." He glanced at Selene and smiled. "There are lots of kids around our camp. We get packages from home and they beg for candy and cookies from us. They don't get many sweets."

"Is there lots of little girls?" Selene asked.

"Now, we don't see many little girls," he told her. "Their customs are very different from ours. The girls mostly stay with their mothers. The boys tag along after their fathers."

"I'd like to tag along with my father," Selene said sadly. "But he went away."

"Away?"

Sassy mouthed "he died," and Caleb nodded quickly.

"Do have some more coffee, Caleb," Mrs. Peale offered.

"Thank you. It's very good."

Sassy had rationed out enough for a pot of the delicious beverage. It was expensive, and they rarely drank it. But Mrs. Peale said that Caleb loved coffee and he had, after all, contributed the meal. Sassy felt that a cup of good coffee wasn't that much of a sacrifice, under the circumstances.

After dinner, they gathered around the television to watch the news. Caleb looked at his watch and said he had to get back to Billings, because his aunt wanted to go to a late movie, and he'd promised to take her.

"But I'd like to come back again before I return to duty, if I may," he told them. "I had a good time tonight."

"So did we," Sassy said at once. "Please do."

"We'll make you a nice macaroni and cheese casserole next time, our treat," Mrs. Peale offered.

He hesitated. "Would you mind if I contributed the cheese for it?" he asked. "I'm partial to a particular brand."

They saw right through him, but they pretended not to. It had to be obvious that they were managing at a subsistence level.

"That would be very kind of you," Mrs. Peale said with genuine gratitude.

He smiled. "It would be my pleasure. Sassy, would you walk me out?"

"Sure!"

She jumped up and walked out to his truck with him. He turned to her before he climbed up into the cab.

"My aunt has a cousin who lives here. She says your mother is in very bad shape," he said.

She nodded. "Lung cancer."

He grimaced. "If there's anything I can do, anything at all," he began. "Your mother was so good to my cousin when she lost her husband in the blizzard a few years ago. None of us have forgotten."

"You're very kind. But we're managing." She grinned. "Thanks for the chicken, I'd forgotten what they tasted like," she added, mimicking her mother's words.

He laughed at her honesty. "You always did have a great sense of humor."

"It's easier to laugh than to cry," she told him.

"So they say. I'll come by tomorrow afternoon, if I may, and tell you when I'm free. My aunt has committed me to no end of social obligations."

"You could phone me," she said.

He grinned. "I'd rather drive over. Humor me. I'll escape tea with one of aunt's friends who has an eligible daughter."

She chuckled. "Avoiding matrimony, are you?"

"Apparently," he agreed. He pursed his lips. "Are you attached?"

She sighed. "No. Sorry." Her eyes widened. "Are you?"

He grimaced. "I'm trying not to be." He shrugged. "She's my best friend's girl."

She relaxed. He wasn't hunting for a woman. "I have one of those situations, too. Except that he doesn't have a girlfriend, that I know of."

"And he doesn't like you?"

"Apparently not."

"Well, if that doesn't take the cake. Two fellow sufferers, and we meet by accident."

"That's life."

"It is." He studied her warmly. "You know, I was

so shy in high school that I never got up the nerve to ask you out. I wanted to. You were always so cheerful, always smiling. You made me feel good inside."

That was surprising. She remembered him as a standoffish young man who seemed never to notice her.

"I was shy, too," she confessed. "I just learned to bluff."

"The Army taught me how to do that," he said, smiling. "This man you're interested in—somebody local?"

She sighed. "Actually, he's sort of the foreman of a ranch. The men he works for bought the old Bradbury place . . ."

"That wreck?" he exclaimed. "Whatever for?"

"They're going to run purebred calves out there, once they build a new barn and stable and remodel the house and run new fences. It's going to be quite a job."

"A very expensive job. Who are his bosses?"

"The Callister brothers. They live in Medicine Ridge."

He nodded. "Yes. I've heard of them. Hard working men. One of their ranch hands was in my unit when I first shipped out. He said it was the best place he'd ever worked." He laughed. "He said the brothers got right out in the pasture at branding time and helped. They weren't the sort to sit in parlors and sip expensive alcohol."

"Imagine, to be that rich and still go out to work cattle," she said with a wistful smile.

"I can't imagine it," he told her. "But I'd love to be able to. I'm getting my college degree in the military. When I come out, I'm going to apprentice at a mechanic's shop in Billings and, hopefully, work my way up to partnership one day. I love fixing motors."

She gave him a wry look. "I wish you'd love fixing mine," she said. "It's pouring black smoke."

"How old is it?" he asked curiously.

"About twenty years . . ."

"Rings and valves," he said at once. "It's probably going to need rebuilding. At today's prices, you'd come out better to sell it for scrap and buy a new one."

"Pipe dreams," she laughed. "We live up to the last penny I bring home. I could never make a car payment."

"Have you thought about moving to Billings, where you could get a better job?"

"I'd have to take Mama and Selene with me," she said simply, "and we'd have to rent a place to live. At least we still have the house, such as it is."

He frowned. "You landed in a fine mess," he said sympathetically.

"I did, indeed. But I love my family," she added. "I'd rather have what I have than be a millionaire."

His dark eyes met her green ones evenly.

"You're a nice girl, Sassy. I wish I'd known you better before I met my best friend's girl."

"I wish I'd known you better before John Taggert came to town," she sighed. "As it is, I'll be very happy to have you for a friend." She grinned. "We can cry on each others' shoulders. I'll even write to you when you go back overseas if you'll give me your address."

His face lit up. "I'd like that. It will help throw my buddy off the trail. He caught me staring at his girlfriend's photo a little too long."

"I'll send you a picture of me," she volunteered. "You can tell him she reminded you of me."

His eyebrows lifted. "That won't be far-fetched. She's dark haired and has light eyes. You'd do that for me?"

"Of course I would," she said easily. "What are friends for?"

He smiled. "Maybe I can do you a good turn one day."

"Maybe you can."

He climbed into the truck. "Tell your family I said good night. I'll drive over tomorrow."

She smiled up at him. "I'll look forward to it."

He threw up a hand and pulled out into the road. She watched him go, remembering that there were still a few pieces of chicken left. She'd have to rush inside and put them up quickly before Selene grew reckless and ate too much. If they stretched out that bucket of chicken, they could eat on it for most of the week. It was a godsend, considering their normal grocery budget. God bless Caleb, she thought warmly. He really did have a big heart.

John Callister had spent a pleasant weekend with his brother and Kasie and the girls. Mrs. Charters had made him his favorite foods, and even Miss Parsons, Gil's former governess who was now his bookkeeper, seemed to enjoy his visit. There was a new secretary since Gil had married Kasie. He was a male secretary, Arnold Sims, who seemed nice and was almost as efficient as Kasie had been. He was an older man, and he and Miss Parsons spent their days off together.

It was nice to get away from the constant headache of construction and back to the bosom of his family. But he had to return to Hollister, and mend fences with Sassy. He should have found a kinder way to keep her at arm's length while he found his footing in their changing relationship. Her face had gone pale when he'd jerked back from her. She probably thought he found her offensive. He hated leaving her with that false impression, but his sudden desire for her had shocked and disturbed him. He hadn't been confident enough to go back and face her until he could hide his feelings.

There had to be some way to make it up to her. He'd think of a way when he got back to Hollister, he assured himself. He could explain it away without too much difficulty. Sassy had a kind heart. He knew she wouldn't hold grudges.

But when he walked into the store Monday afternoon, he got a shock. Sassy was leaning over the counter, smiling broadly at a very handsome young man in jeans and a chambray shirt. And if he wasn't mistaken, the young man was holding her hand.

He felt something inside him explode with pain and resentment. She'd put her hands on his chest and looked up at him with melting green eyes, and he'd wanted her to the point of madness. Now she was doing the same thing to another man, a younger man. Was she just a heartless flirt?

He walked up to the counter, noting idly that the younger man didn't seem to be disturbed by him, or even interested in him.

"Hi, Sassy," he said coolly. "Did you get in that special feed mix I asked you to order?"

"I'll check, Mr. Taggert," she said politely and with a quiet smile. She walked into the back to check the invoice of the latest shipment that had just come that morning, very proud that she'd been able to disguise her quick breathing and shaky legs. John Taggert had a shattering effect on her emotions. But he didn't want her, and she'd better remember it. What a blessing that Caleb had come to the store today. Perhaps John would believe that she had other interests and wasn't chasing after him.

"Nice day," John said to the young man. "I'm John Taggert. I'll be ramrodding the old Bradbury ranch."

The boy smiled and extended a hand. "I'm Caleb Danner. Sassy and I went to school together."

John shook the hand. "Nice to meet you."

"Same here."

John looked around at the shelves with seeming nonchalance. "You work around here?" he asked carelessly.

"No. I'm in the Army Rangers," the boy replied, surprising his companion. "I'm stationed overseas, but I've been home on leave for a couple of weeks. I'm staying with my aunt in Billings."

John's pale eyes met the boy's dark ones. "That's a substantial drive from here."

"Yes, I know," Caleb replied easily. "But I promised Sassy a movie and I'm free tonight. I came to see if she'd go with me."

CHAPTER SIX

THE boy was an Army Ranger he said, and he was dating Sassy. John felt uncomfortable trying to pump the younger man for information. He wondered if Caleb was seriously interested in Sassy, but he had no right to ask.

She was poring over bills of lading. He watched her with muted curiosity and a little jealousy. It disturbed him that this younger man had popped up right out of the ground, so to speak, under his own nose.

It took her a minute to find the order and calm her nerves. But she managed to do both. She looked up as John approached the counter. He looked very sexy in those well-fitting jeans and the blue-checked Western-cut shirt he was wearing with his black boots and wide-brimmed hat. She shouldn't notice that, she told herself firmly. He wouldn't like having her interested in him; he'd already made that clear. She had to be businesslike.

"The feed was backordered," she said politely. "But it should be here by Friday, if that's all right. If it isn't," she added quickly when he began to look irritated, "I can ask Mr. Mannheim to phone them . . ."

"No need," he said abruptly. "We can wait. We aren't moving livestock onto the place until we have the fences mended and the barn finished. I just want to have the feed on hand when they arrive."

"We'll have it by next week. No problem."

He nodded. He tried to avoid looking at her directly. She was wearing jeans with a neat little white peasant blouse that had embroidery on it, and she looked very pretty with her dark hair crisp and clean, and her green eyes shimmering with pleasure. Her face was flushed and she was obviously unsettled. The boy at the counter probably had something to do with that, he thought irritably. She seemed pretty wrapped up in him already.

"That's fine," he said abruptly. "I'll check back with you next week, or I'll have one of the boys come in."

"Yes, sir," she replied politely.

He nodded at Caleb and stalked out of the store without another glance at Sassy.

Caleb pursed his lips and noted Sassy's heightened color. "So that's him," he mused.

She drew in a steadying breath. "That's him."

"Talk about biting off more than you can chew," he murmured dryly.

"What do you mean?"

"Nothing," he returned, thinking privately that Taggert looked like a man who'd forgotten more about women than Sassy would ever learn about men. Taggert seemed sophisticated, for a cattleman, and was obviously used to giving orders. Sassy was too young for that fire-eater, too unsophisticated, too everything. Besides all that, the ranch foreman had spoken to her politely, but in a manner that was decidedly impersonal. Caleb didn't want to upset Sassy by putting all that into words. Still, he felt sympathy for her. She was as likely to land that big fish as he was to find himself out on the town with his best friend's girl.

"How about that movie?" he asked quickly, changing the subject. "The local theater has three new ones showing . . ."

• • •

They went to Hollister's only in-town movie theater, a small building in town that did a pretty good business catering to families. There was a drive-in movie on the outskirts of town, in a cow-pasture, but Caleb wasn't keen on that, so they went into town.

The movie they chose was a cartoon movie about a robot, and it was hilarious. Sassy had worried about leaving her mother and Selene alone, but Mrs. Peale refused to let her sacrifice a night out. Sassy did leave her prepaid cell phone with her mother, though, in case of an emergency. Caleb had one of his own, so they could use it if they were in any difficulties.

Caleb drove her back home. He had a nice truck; it wasn't new, but it was well-maintained. He was sending home the payments to his aunt, who was making them for him.

"I only have a year to go," he told her. "Yesterday, I got a firm offer of a partnership in Billings at a cousin's car dealership. He has a shop that does mechanical work. I'd be in charge of that, and do bodywork as well. I went by to see him on a whim, and he offered me the job, just like that." His dark eyes twinkled. "It's what I've wanted to do my whole life."

"I hope you make it," she told him with genuine feeling.

He bent and kissed her cheek. "You're a nice girl, Sassy," he said softly. "I wish . . ."

"Me, too," she said, reading the thought in his face. "But life makes other plans, sometimes."

"Doesn't it?" he chuckled.

"When do you report back to duty?" she asked.

"Not for a week, but my aunt has every minute scheduled. She had plans for tonight, too, but I outfoxed her," he said, grinning.

"I enjoyed the movie. And the chicken," she told him.

"I enjoyed the macaroni and cheese we had tonight," he replied. He was somber for a minute. "If you ever need help, I hope you'll ask me. I'd do what I can for you."

She smiled up at him. "I know that. Thanks, Caleb. I'd make the same offer. But," she sighed, "I have no clue what I'd ever be able to help you with."

"I'll send you my address," he said, having already jotted hers down on a piece of paper. "You can send me that photo, to throw my buddy off the track."

She laughed. "Okay. I'll definitely do that."

"I'll phone you before I leave. Take care."

"You, too. So long."

He got into his truck and drove away.

Sassy walked slowly up the porch and into the house, her mind still on the funny movie.

She was halfway into the living room when she realized that one of the muffled voices she'd been hearing was male.

As she entered the room, John Taggert looked up from the sofa, where he was sitting with her mother. Her mother, she noted, was grinning like a Cheshire cat.

"Mr. Taggert came by to see how I was doing. Wasn't that sweet of him?" she asked her daughter.

"It really was," Sassy replied politely.

"Had a good time?" John asked her. He wasn't smiling.

"Yes," she said. "It was a cartoon movie."

"Just right for children," he replied, and there was something in his blue eyes that made her heart jump.

"We're all children at heart. I'm sure that's what you meant, wasn't it, Mr. Taggert?" Mrs. Peale asked sweetly.

He caught himself. "Of course," he replied, smiling at the older woman. "I enjoy them myself. We take the girls to movies all the time."

"Girls?" Mrs. Peale asked, frowning.

"My nieces," he explained. "They love cartoons. My brother and his wife take them mostly, but I fill in when I'm needed."

"You like children?"

He smiled. "I love them."

Mrs. Peale opened her mouth.

Sassy knew what was coming, so she jumped in. "Caleb's going to phone us before he goes back overseas," she told her mother.

"That's nice of him." Mrs. Peale beamed. "Such a kind young man."

"Kind." Sassy nodded.

"Would you like something to drink, Mr. Taggert?" Mrs. Peale asked politely. "Sassy could make some coffee . . . ?"

John glanced at his watch. "I've got to go. Thanks anyway. I just wanted to make sure you were all right," he told Mrs. Peale, and he smiled at her. "Sassy's . . . boyfriend mentioned that he was taking her to a movie, and I thought about you out here all alone."

Sassy gave him a glare hot enough to scald. "I left Mama my cell phone in case anything happened," she said curtly.

"Yes, she did," Mrs. Peale added quickly. "She takes very good care of me. I insisted that she go with Caleb. Sassy hasn't had a night out in two or three years."

John shifted, as if that statement made him uneasy.

"She doesn't like to leave me at all," Mrs. Peale continued. "But it's not fair to her. So much responsibility, and at her age."

"I never mind it," Sassy interrupted. "I love you."

"I know that, sweetheart, but you should get to know nice young men," she added. "You'll marry one day and have children. You can't spend your whole life like this, with a sick old woman and a child . . ."

"Please," Sassy said, hurting. "I don't want to think about getting married for years yet."

Mrs. Peale's face mirrored her sorrow. "You should never have had to handle this all alone," she said regretfully. "If only your father had . . . well, that's not something we could help."

"I'll walk Mr. Taggert to the door," Sassy offered. She looked as if she'd like to drag him out it, before her mother could embarrass her even more.

"Am I leaving?" he asked Sassy.

"Apparently," she replied, standing aside and nodding toward the front door.

"In that case, I'll say good night." He smiled at Mrs. Peale. "I hope you know that you can call on me if you ever needed help. I'm not in the Army, but I do have skills that don't involve an intimate knowledge of guns—"

"This way, Mr. Taggert." Sassy interrupted emphatically, catching him firmly by the sleeve.

He grinned at Mrs. Peale, whose eyes were twinkling now. "Good night."

"Good night, Mr. Taggert. Thank you for stopping by."

"You're very welcome."

He followed Sassy out onto the front porch. She closed the door.

His eyebrows arched. "Why did you close the door?" he asked. His voice deepened with amusement. "Are you going to kiss me good night and you don't want your mother to see?"

She flushed. "I wouldn't kiss you for all the tea in China! There's no telling where you've been!"

"Actually," he said, twirling his wide-brimmed hat in his big hands, "I've been in Medicine Ridge, reporting to my bosses."

"That's nice. Do drive safely on your way back to your ranch."

He stopped twirling the hat and studied her stiff posture. He felt between a rock and a hard place.

"The Army Ranger seems like a good sort of boy," he remarked. "Responsible. Not very mature yet, but he'll grow up."

She wanted to bite him. "He's in the Army Rangers," she reminded him. "He's been in combat overseas."

His eyebrows lifted. "Is that a requirement for your dates, that they've learned to dodge bullets?"

"I never said I wanted a man who could dodge bullets!" she threw at him.

"It might be a handy skill for a man—dodging things, I mean, if you're the sort of woman who likes to throw pots and pans at men."

"I have never thrown a pot at a man," she said emphatically. "However, if you'd like to step into our kitchen, I could make an exception for you!"

He grinned. He could have bet that she didn't talk like that to the soldier boy. She had spirit and she didn't take guff from anyone, but it took a lot to get under her skin. It delighted him that he could make her mad.

"What sort of pot did you have in mind throwing at me?" he taunted.

"Something made of cast iron," she muttered. "Although I expect you'd dent it."

"My head is not that hard," he retorted.

He stepped in, close to her, and watched her reaction with detached amusement. He made her nervous. It showed.

He put his hat back on, and pushed it to the back of his head. One long arm went around Sassy's waist and drew her to him. A big, lean hand spread on her cheek, coaxing it back to his shoulder.

"You've got grit," he murmured deeply as his gaze fell to her soft mouth. "You don't back away from trouble, or responsibility. I like that."

"You . . . shouldn't hold me like this," she protested weakly.

"Why not? You're soft and sweet and I like the way you smell." His head began to bend. "I think I'll like the way you taste, too," he breathed.

He didn't need a program to know how innocent she was. He loved the way her hands gripped him, almost in fear, as his firm mouth smoothed over the parted, shocked warmth of her lips.

"Nothing heavy," he whispered as his mouth played with hers. "It's far too soon for that. Relax. Just relax, Sassy. It's like dancing, slow and sweet . . ."

His mouth covered hers gently, brushing her lips apart, teasing them to permit the slow invasion. Her hands relaxed their death-grip on his arms as the slow rhythm began to increase her heartbeat and make her breathing sound jerky and rough. He was very good at this, she thought dizzily. He knew exactly how to make her shiver with anticipation as he drew out the intimate torture of his mouth on her lips. He teased them, playing with her lower lip, nibbling and rubbing, until she went on tiptoe with a frustrated moan, seeking something far rougher and more passionate than this exquisite whisper of motion.

He nipped her lower lip. "You want more, don't you, honey?" he whispered roughly. "So do I. Hold tight."

Her hands slid up to his broad shoulders as his mouth began to burrow hungrily into hers. She let her lips open with a shiver, closing her eyes and reaching up to be swallowed whole by his arms.

It was so sweet that she moaned with the ardent passion he aroused in her. She'd never felt her body swell and shudder like this when a man held her. She'd never been kissed so thoroughly, so expertly. Her arms tightened convulsively around his neck as he riveted her to the length of his powerful body, as if he, too, had lost control of himself.

A minute later, he came to his senses. She was just nineteen. She worked for him, even though she didn't know it. They were worlds apart in every way. What the hell was he doing?

He pulled away from her abruptly, his blue eyes shimmering with emotion, his grasp a little bruising as he tried to get his breath back under control. His jealousy of the soldier had pushed him right into a situation he'd left town to avoid. Now, here he was, faced with the consequences.

She hung there, watching him with clouded, dreamy eyes in a face flushed with pleasure from the hungry exchange.

"That was a mistake," he said curtly, putting her firmly at arm's length and letting her go.

"Are you sure?" she asked, dazed.

"Yes, I'm sure," he said, his voice sharp with anger.

"Then why did you do it?" she asked reasonably.

He had to think about a suitable answer, and his brain wasn't working very well. He'd pushed her away at their last meeting and felt guilt. Now he'd compounded the error and he couldn't think of a good way to get out of it.

"God knows," he said heavily. "Maybe it's the full moon."

She gave him a wry look. "It's not a full moon. It's a crescent moon."

"A moon is a moon," he said doggedly.

"That's your story and you're sticking to it," she agreed.

He stared down at her with conflict eating him alive. "You're nineteen, Sassy," he said finally. "I'm thirty-one."

She blinked. "Is that supposed to mean something?"

"It means you're years too young for me. And not only in age."

She raised her eyebrows. "It isn't exactly easy to get experience when you're living in a tiny town and supporting a family."

He ground his teeth. "That isn't the point . . ."

She held up a hand. "You had too much coffee today and the caffeine caused you to leap on unsuspecting women."

He glowered. "I did not drink too much coffee."

"Then it must be either my exceptional beauty or my overwhelming charm," she decided. She waited, arms folded, for him to come up with an alternate theory.

He pulled his hat low over his eyes. "It's been a long, dry spell."

"Well, if that isn't the nicest compliment I ever had," she muttered. "You were lonely and I was the only eligible woman handy!"

"You were," he shot back.

"A likely story! There's Mrs. Harmon, who lives a mile down the road."

"Mrs. Harmon?"

"Yes. Her husband has been dead fifteen years. She's fifty, but she wears tight skirts and a lot of makeup and in dim light, she isn't half bad."

He glowered even more. "I am not that desperate."

"You just said you were."

"I did not!"

"Making passes at nineteen-year-old girls," she scoffed. "I never!"

He threw up his hands. "It wasn't a pass!"

She pursed her lips and gave him a sarcastic look.

He shrugged. "Maybe it was a small pass." He stuck his hands in his pockets. "I have a conscience. You'd wear on it."

So that was why he'd pushed her away in the store, before he left town. Her heart lifted. He didn't find her unattractive. He just thought she was too young.

"I'll be twenty next month," she told him.

It didn't help. "I'll be thirty-two in two months."

"Well, for a month we'll be almost the same age," she said pertly.

He laughed shortly. "Twelve years is a lot, at your age."

"In the great scheme of things, it isn't," she pointed out.

He didn't answer her.

"Thanks for stopping by to check on my mother," she said. "It was kind."

He lifted a shoulder. "I wanted to see if the soldier was hot for you."

"Excuse me?!"

"He didn't even kiss you good night," he said.

"That's because he's in love with his best friend's girl."

His expression brightened. "He is?"

"I'm somebody to talk about her with," she told him. "Which is why I don't get out much, unless a man wants to tell me about his love life and ask for advice." She studied him. "I don't guess you've got relationship problems?"

"In fact, I do. I'm trying not to have one with an inappropriate woman," he said, tongue-in-cheek.

That took a minute to register. She laughed. "Oh. I see."

He moved closer and toyed with a strand of her short hair. "I guess it wouldn't hurt to take you out once in a while. Nothing serious," he added firmly. "I am not in the market for a mistress."

"Good thing," she returned, "because I have no intention of becoming one."

He grinned. "Now, that's encouraging. I'm glad to know that you have enough willpower to keep us on the straight and narrow."

"I have my mother," she replied, "who would shoot you in the foot with a rusty gun if she even thought you were leading me into a life of sin. She's very religious. She raised me to be that way."

"In her condition," he said solemnly, "I'm not surprised that she's religious. She's a courageous soul."

"I love her a lot," she confessed. "I wish I could do more to help her."

"Loving her is probably what helps her the most," he said. He bent and brushed a soft kiss against her mouth. "I'll see you tomorrow."

She smiled. "Okay."

He started to walk down the steps, paused, and

turned back to her. "You're sure it's not serious with the soldier?"

She smiled more broadly. "Very sure."

He cocked his hat at a jaunty angle and grinned at her. "Okay."

She watched him walk out to his vehicle, climb in, and drive away. She waved, but she noticed that he didn't look back. For some reason, that bothered her.

John spent a rough night remembering how sweet Sassy was to kiss. He'd been fighting the attraction for weeks now, and he was losing. She was too young for him. He knew it. But on the other hand, she was independent. She was strong. She was used to responsibility. She'd had years of being the head of her family, the breadwinner. She might be young, but she was more mature than most women her age.

He could see how much care she took for her mother and her mother's little ward. She never shirked her duties, and she worked hard for her paycheck.

The bottom line was that he was far too attracted to her to walk away. He was taking a chance. But he'd taken chances before in his life, with women who were much inferior to this little firecracker. It wouldn't hurt to go slow and see where the path led. After all, he could walk away whenever he liked, he told himself.

The big problem was going to be the distance between them socially. Sassy didn't know that he came from great wealth, that his parents were related to most of the royal houses of Europe, that he and his brother had built a world-famous ranch that bred equally famous breeding bulls. He was used to five-star hotels and restaurants, stretch limousines in every city he visited. He traveled first-class. He was worldly and sophisticated. Sassy was much more used to small town life. She wouldn't understand his world. Probably, she wouldn't be able to adjust to it.

But he was creating hurdles that didn't exist yet. It wasn't as if he was in love with her and aching to rush her to the altar, he told himself. He was going to take her out a few times. Maybe kiss her once in a while. It was nothing he couldn't handle. She'd just be companionship while he was getting this new ranching enterprise off the ground. When he had to leave, he'd tell her the truth.

It sounded simple. It was simple, he assured himself. She was just another girl, another casual relationship. He was going to enjoy it while it lasted.

He went to sleep, finally, having resolved all the problems in his mind.

The next day, he went back to the feed store with another list, this one of household goods that he was going to need. He was looking forward to seeing Sassy again. The memory of that kiss had prompted some unusually spicy dreams about her.

But when he got there, he found Buck Mannheim handling the counter and looking worried.

He waited while the older man finished a sale. The customer left and John approached the counter.

"Where's Sassy?" he asked.

Buck looked concerned. "She phoned me at home. Her mother had a bad turn. They had to send an ambulance for her and take her up to Billings to the nearest hospital. Sassy was crying . . ."

He was talking to thin air. John was already out the door.

He found Sassy and little Selene in the emergency waiting room, huddled together and upset.

He walked into the room and they both ran to him, to be scooped up and held close, comforted.

He felt odd. It was the first time he could remember being important to anyone outside his own family circle. He felt needed.

His arms contracted around them. "Tell me what happened," he asked at Sassy's ear.

She drew away a little, wiping at her eyes with the hem of her blouse. It was obvious that she hadn't slept. "She knocked over her water carafe, or I wouldn't even have known anything was wrong. I ran in to see what had happened and I found her gasping for breath. It was so bad that I just ran to the phone and called Dr. Bates. He sent for the ambulance and called the oncologist on staff here. They've been with her for two hours. Nobody's told me anything."

He eased them down into chairs. "Stay here," he said softly. "I'll find out what's going on."

She was doubtful that a cowboy, even a foreman, would be able to elicit more information than the patient's own family, but she smiled. "Thanks."

He turned and walked down the hall.

CHAPTER SEVEN

JOHN had money and power, and he knew how to use both. Within two minutes, he'd been ushered into the office of the hospital administrator. He explained who he was, why he was there, and asked for information. Even in Billings, the Callister empire was known. Five minutes later, he was speaking to the physician in charge of Sassy's mother's case. He accepted responsibility for the bill and asked if anything more could be done than was being done.

"Sadly, yes," the physician said curtly. "We're bound by the family's financial constraints. Mrs. Peale does have insurance, but she told us that they simply could not afford anything other than symptomatic relief for her. If she would consent, Mrs. Peale could have surgery to remove the cancerous lung and then radiation and chemotherapy to insure her recovery. In fact, she'd have a very good prognosis . . ."

"If money's all that's holding things up, I'll gladly be responsible for the bill. I don't care how much it is. So what are you waiting for?" John asked.

The physician smiled. "You'll speak to the financial officer?"

"Immediately," he replied.

"Then I'll speak to the patient."

"They don't know who I am," John told him. "That's the only condition, that you don't tell them. They think I'm the foreman of a ranch."

The older man frowned. "Is there a reason?"

"Originally, it was to insure that costs didn't escalate locally because the name was known," he said. "But by then, it was too late to change things. They're my friends," he added. "I don't want them to look at me differently."

"You think they would?"

"People see fame and money and power. They don't see people. Not at first."

The other man nodded. "I think I understand. I'll get the process underway. It's a very kind thing you're doing," he added. "Mrs. Peale would have died. Very soon, too."

"I know that. She's a good person."

"And very important to her little family, from what I've seen."

"Yes."

He clapped John on the shoulder. "We'll do everything possible."

"Thanks."

• • •

When he wrapped up things in the financial office, he strolled back down to the emergency room. Sassy was pacing the floor. Selene had curled up into a chair with her cheek pillowed on her arm. She was sound asleep.

Sassy met him, her eyes wide and fascinated. "What did you *do?*" she exclaimed. "They're going to operate on Mama! The doctor says they can save her life, that she can have radiation and chemotherapy, that there's a grant for poor people . . . she can live!"

Her voice broke into tears. John pulled her close and rocked her in his strong, warm arms, his mouth against her temple. "It's all right, honey," he said softly. "Don't cry."

"I'm just so happy," she choked at his chest. "So happy! I never knew there were such things as grants for this sort of thing, or I'd have done anything to find one! I thought . . . I thought we'd have to watch her die . . ."

"Never while there was a breath in my body," he whispered. His arms contracted. A wave of feeling rippled through him. He'd helped people in various ways all his life, but it was the first time he'd been able to make this sort of difference for someone he cared about. He'd grown fond of Mrs. Peale. But he'd thought that her case was hopeless. He thanked God that the emergency had forced Sassy to bring her mother here. What a wonderful near-tragedy. A link in a chain that would lead to a better life for all three of them.

She drew back, wiping her eyes again and laughing. "Sorry. I seem to spend my life crying. I'm just so grateful. What did you do?" she asked again.

He grinned. "I just asked wasn't there something they could figure out to do to help her. The doctor said he'd check, and he came up with the grant."

She shook her head. "It happened so fast. They've got some crackerjack surgeon who's teaching new techniques in cancer intervention here, and he's the one they're getting to operate on Mama. What's more, they're going to do it tomorrow. They already asked her, and she just almost jumped out of the bed she was so excited." She wiped away more tears. "We brought her up here to die," she explained. "And it was the most wonderful, scary experience we ever had. She's going to live, maybe long enough to see Selene graduate from college!"

He smiled down at her. "You know, I wouldn't be surprised at all if that's not the case. Feel better?"

She nodded. Her eyes adored him. "Thank you."

He chuckled. "Glad I could help." He glanced down at Selene, who was radiant. "Hear that? You'll have to go to college."

She grinned. "I want to be a doctor, now."

"There are scholarships that will help that dream come true, at the right time," he assured her.

Sassy pulled the young girl close. "We'll find lots," she promised.

"Thank you for helping save our mama," Selene told John solemnly. "We love her very much."

"She loves you very much," John replied. "That must be pretty nice, at your age."

He was saying something without saying it.

Sassy sent Selene to the vending machines for apple juice. While she was gone, Sassy turned to John. "What was your mother like when you were little?"

His face hardened. "I didn't have a mother when I was little," he replied curtly. "My brother and I were raised by our uncle."

She was shocked. "Were your parents still alive?"

"Yes. But they didn't want us."

"How horrible!"

He averted his eyes. "We had a rough upbringing. Until our uncle took us in, we were in—" he started to say boarding school, but that was a dead giveaway "—in a bad situation at home," he amended. "Our uncle took us with him and we grew up without a mother's influence."

"You still don't have anything to do with her? Or your father?"

"We started seeing them again last year," he said after a minute. "It's been hard. We built up resentments and barriers. But we're all working on it. Years too late," he added on a cold laugh.

"I'm sorry," she told him. "Mama's been there for me all my life. She's kissed my cuts and bruises, loved me, fought battles for me . . . I don't know what I would have done without her."

He drew in a long breath and looked down into warm green eyes. "I would have loved having a mother like her," he said honestly. "She's the most optimistic person I ever knew. In her condition, that says a lot."

"I thought we'd be planning her funeral when we came in here," Sassy said, still shell-shocked.

He touched her soft cheek gently. "I can understand that."

"How did you know where we were?" she asked suddenly.

"I went into the feed store with a list and found Buck holding down the fort," he said. "He said you were up here."

"And you came right away," she said, amazed.

He put both big hands on her small waist and held her in front of him. His blue eyes were solemn. "I never planned to get mixed up with you," he told her honestly. "Or your family. But I seem to be part of it."

She smiled. "Yes. You are a part of our family."

His hands contracted. "I just want to make the point that my interest isn't brotherly," he added.

The look in his eyes made her heartbeat accelerate. "Really?"

He smiled. "Really."

She felt as if she could fly. The expression on her face made him wish that they were in a more private place. He looked down to her full mouth and contemplated something shocking and potentially embarrassing.

Before he could act on what was certainly a crazy impulse, the doctor who'd admitted Mrs. Peale came walking up to them with a taller, darker man. He introduced himself and his companion.

"Miss Peale, this is Dr. Barton Crowley," he told Sassy. "He's going to operate on your mother first thing in the morning."

Sassy shook his hand warmly. "I'm so glad to meet you. We're just overwhelmed. We thought we'd brought Mama up here to die. It's a miracle! We never even knew there were grants for surgery!"

John shot a warning look at the doctor and the surgeon, who nodded curtly. The hospital administrator had already told them about the financial arrangements.

"We can always find a way to handle critical situations here," the doctor said with a smile. He nodded toward Dr. Crowley. "He's been teaching us new surgical techniques. It really was a miracle that he was here when you arrived. He works at Johns Hopkins, you see," he added.

Sassy didn't know what that meant.

John leaned down. "It's one of the more famous hospitals back East," he told her.

She laughed nervously. "Sorry," she told Dr. Crowley, who smiled. "I don't get out much."

"She works at our local feed store," John told them, beaming down at her. "She's the family's only support. She takes care of her mother and their six-year-old ward as well. She's quite a girl."

"Stop that," Sassy muttered shyly. "I'm not some paragon of virtue. I love my family."

His eyebrows arched and his eyes twinkled. "All of it?" he asked amusedly.

She flushed when she recalled naming him part of the family. She forced her attention back to the surgeon. "You really think you can help Mama? Our local doctor said the cancer was very advanced."

"It is, but preliminary tests indicate that it's confined to one lobe of her lung. If we can excise it, then follow up with chemotherapy and radiation, there's a good chance that we can at least prolong her life. We might save it altogether."

"Please do whatever you can," Sassy pleaded gently. "She means so much to us."

"She was very excited when I spoke with her," Dr. Crowley said with a smile. "She was concerned about her daughters, she told me, much more than with her own condition. A most unique lady."

"Yes, she is," Sassy agreed. "She's always putting other people's needs in front of her own. She raised me with hardly any help at all, and it was rough."

"From what I see, young woman," the surgeon replied, "she did a very good job."

"Thanks," she said, a little embarrassed.

"Well, we'll get her into surgery first thing. When we see the extent of the cancerous tissue, we'll speak again. Try to get some rest."

"We will."

He and the doctor shook hands with John and walked back down the hall.

"I wish I'd packed a blanket or something," Sassy mused, eyeing the straight, lightly padded chairs in the distant waiting room. "I can sleep sitting up, but it gets cold in hospitals."

"Sitting up?" He didn't understand.

"Listen, you know how we're fixed," she said. "We can't afford a motel room. I always sleep in the waiting room when Mama's in the hospital." She nodded toward Selene, who was now asleep in the corner. "We both do it. Except Selene fits in these chairs a little better, because she's so small."

He was shocked. It was a firsthand look at how the rest of the world had to live. He hadn't realized that Sassy would have to stay at the hospital.

"Don't look like that," she said. "You make me uncomfortable. I don't mind being poor. I've got so many blessings that it's hard to count them."

"Blessings." He frowned, as if he wondered what they could possibly be.

"I have a mother who sacrificed to raise me, who loves me with her whole heart. I have a little sort-of sister who thinks I'm Joan of Arc. I have a roof over my head, food to eat, and, thanks to you, a really good job with no harassment tied to it. I even have a vehicle that gets me to and from work most of the time."

"I wouldn't call that vehicle a blessing," he observed.

"Neither would I, if I could afford that fancy truck you drive," she chided, grinning. "The point is, I have things that a lot of other people don't. I'm happy," she added, curious about his expression.

She had nothing. Literally nothing. But she could count her blessings as if they made her richer than a princess. He had everything, but his life was empty. All the wealth and power he commanded hadn't made him happy. He was alone. He had Gil and his family, and his parents. But in a very personal sense, he was by himself.

"You're thinking that you don't really have a family of your own," Sassy guessed from his glum expression. "But you do. You have me, and Mama, and Selene. We're your family." She hesitated, because he looked hunted. She flushed. "I know we're not much to brag about . . ."

His arm shot out and pulled her to him. "Don't run yourself down. I've never counted my friends by their bank books. Character is far more important."

She relaxed. But only a little. He was very close, and her heart was racing.

"You suit me just the way you are," he said gently. He bent and kissed her, tenderly, before he let her go and walked toward Selene.

"What are you doing?" she exclaimed when he lifted the sleeping child in his arms and started toward the exit.

"I'm taking baby sister here to a modest guest room for the night. You can come, too."

She blinked. "John, I can't afford—"

"If I hear that one more time," he interrupted, "I'm going to say bad words. You don't want me to say bad words in front of the child. Do you?"

She was asleep and wouldn't hear them, but he was making a point and being noble. She gave in, smiling. "Okay. But you have to dock my wages for it or I'll stay here and Selene can just hear you spout bad words."

He smiled over Selene's head on his chest. "Okay, honey."

The word brought a soft blush into Sassy's cheeks and he chuckled softly. He led the way out the door to his truck.

John's idea of a modest guest room was horrifying to Sassy when he stopped by the desk of Billings's best hotel to check in Sassy and Selene.

The child stirred sleepily in John's strong arms.

She opened her eyes, yawning. “Mama?” she exclaimed, worried.

“She’s fine,” John assured her. “Go back to sleep, baby. Curl up in this chair until I get the formalities done, okay?” He placed her gently into a big, cushy armchair near the desk.

“Okay, John,” Selene said, smiling as she closed her eyes and nodded off again.

“You’d better stay with her while I do this,” John told Sassy, not wanting her to hear the clerk when he gave her his real name to pay for the room.

“Okay, John,” she echoed her little sister, with a grin.

He winked at her and went back to the desk. The smile faded as he spoke to the male clerk.

“Their mother is in the hospital, about to have cancer surgery. They were going to sleep in the waiting room. I want a room for them, near mine, if it’s possible.”

The clerk, a kindly young man, smiled sympathetically. “There’s one adjoining yours, Mr. Callister,” he said politely. “It’s a double. Would that do?”

“Yes.”

The clerk made the arrangements, took John’s credit card, processed the transaction, handed back the card, and then went to program the card-key for the new guests. He was back in no time, very efficient.

“I hope their mother does all right,” he told John.

"So do I. But she's in very good hands."

He went back to Selene, lifted her gently, and motioned to Sassy, who was examining the glass coffee table beside the chairs.

She paused at a pillar as they walked into the elevator. "Gosh, this looks like real marble," she murmured, and then had to run to make it before the elevator doors closed. "John, this place looks expensive . . ."

"I'll make sure to tell Buck to dock your salary over several months, okay?" he asked gently, and he smiled.

She was apprehensive. It was going to be a big chunk of her income. But he'd already been so nice that she felt guilty for even making a fuss. "Sure, that's fine."

He led them down the hall and gave Sassy the card-key to insert in the lock. She stared at it.

"Why are you giving me a credit card?" she asked in all honesty.

He gaped at her. "It's the door key."

She cocked an eyebrow. "Right." She looked up at him as if she expected men with white nets to appear.

He laughed when he realized she hadn't a clue about modern technology. "Give it here."

He balanced Selene on one lifted knee, inserted the card, jerked it back out so the green light on the lock blinked, and then opened the door.

Sassy's jaw dropped.

"It's a card-key," he repeated, leading the way in.

Sassy closed the door behind them, turning on the lights as she went. The room was a revelation. There was a huge new double bed—two of them, in fact. There were paintings on the wall. There was a round table with two chairs. There was a telephone. There was a huge glass window, curtained, that looked out over Billings. There was even a huge television.

"This is a palace," Sassy murmured, spellbound as she looked around. She peered into the bathroom and actually gasped. "There's a hair dryer right here in the room!" she exclaimed.

John had put Selene down gently on one of the double beds. He felt two inches high. Sassy's life had been spent in a small rural town in abject poverty. She knew nothing of high living. Even this hotel, nice but not the five-star accommodation he'd frequented in his travels both in this country and overseas, was opulent to her. Considering where, and how, she and her family lived, this must have seemed like kingly extravagance.

He walked back to the bathroom and leaned against the door facing while she explored tiny wrapped packets of soap and little bottles of shampoo and soap.

"Wow," she whispered.

She touched the thick white towels, so plush that she wanted to wrap up in one. She compared them to her thin, tatty, worn towels at home and was shocked at the contrast. She glanced at John shyly.

"Sorry," she said. "I'm not used to this sort of place."

"It's just a hotel, Sassy," he said softly. "If you've never stayed in one, I imagine it's surprising at first."

"How did you know?" she asked.

"Know what?"

"That I'd never stayed in a hotel?"

He cleared his throat. "Well, it shows. Sort of."

She flushed. "You mean, I'm acting like an idiot."

"I mean nothing of the sort." He shouldered away from the door facing, caught her by the waist, pulled her close, and bent to kiss the breath out of her.

She held on tight, relieved about her mother, but worried about the surgery, and grateful for John's intervention.

"You've made miracles for us," she said when he let her go.

He searched her shimmering green eyes. "You've made one for me," he replied, and he wasn't kidding.

"I have? How?"

His hands contracted on her small waist. "Let's just say, you've taught me about the value of small blessings. I tend to take things for granted, I guess." His eyes narrowed. "You appreciate the most basic things in life. You're so . . . optimistic,

Sassy," he added. "You make me feel humble."

"Oh, that's rich," she chuckled. "A backwoods hick like me making a sophisticated gentleman like you feel humble."

"I'm not kidding," he replied. "You don't have a lot of material things. But you're happy without them." He shrugged. "I've got a lot more than you have, and I'm . . ." He searched for the word, frowning. "I'm . . . empty," he said finally, meeting her quiet eyes.

"But you're the kindest man I've ever known," she argued. "You do things for people without even thinking twice what problems you may cause yourself in the process. You're a good person."

Her wide-eyed fascination made him tingle inside. In recent years, women had wanted him because he was rich and powerful. Here was one who wanted him because he was kind. It was an eye-opener.

"You look strange," she remarked.

"I was thinking," he said.

"About what?"

"About how late it is, and how much you're going to need some sleep. We'll get an early start tomorrow," he told her.

The horror came back, full force. The joy drained out of her face, to be replaced with fear and uncertainty.

He drew her close and rocked her in his arms, bending his head over hers. "That surgeon is rather famous," he said conversationally. "He's one of the best oncologists in the country, and it's a blessing that he ended up here just when your mother needed him. You have to believe that she's going to be all right."

"I'm trying to," she said. "It's just hard. We've had so many trips to the hospital," she confessed, and sounded weary.

John had never had to go through this with his family. Well, there was Gil's first wife who died in a riding accident. That had been traumatic. But since then, John had never worried about losing a relative to disease. He had, he decided, been very lucky.

"I'll be right there with you," he promised her. "All the time."

She drew back and looked up at him with fascinated eyes. "You will? You mean it? Won't you get in trouble with your boss?"

"I won't," he said. "But it wouldn't matter if I did. I'm not leaving you. Not for anything."

She colored and smiled at him.

"After all," he teased, "I'm a member of the family."

She smiled even more.

"Kissing kin," he added, and bent to brush a whisper of a kiss over her soft mouth. He forced himself to step away from her. "Go to bed."

"Okay. Thanks, John. Thanks for everything."

He didn't answer her. He just winked.

• • •

The surgery took several hours. Sassy bit her fingernails off into the quick. Selene sat very close to her, holding her hand.

"I don't want Mama to die," she said.

Sassy pulled her close. "She won't die," she promised. "She's going to get better. I promise." She prayed it wasn't going to be a lie.

John had gone to check with the surgical desk. He came back grinning.

"Tell me!" Sassy exclaimed.

"They were able to get all the cancerous tissue," he said. "It was confined to a lobe of her lung, as he suspected. They're cautiously optimistic that your mother will recover and begin to lead a full life again."

"Oh, my goodness!" Sassy exclaimed, hugging Selene close. "She'll get better!"

Selene hugged her back. "I'm so happy!"

"So am I."

Sassy let her go, got up, and went to hug John close, laying her cheek against his broad, warm chest. He enveloped her in his arms. She felt right at home there.

"Thank you," she murmured.

"For what?"

She looked up at him. "For everything."

He smiled at her, his eyes crinkling.

"What happens now?" she asked.

"Your mother recovers enough to go home, then

we bring her back up here for the treatments. Dr. Crowley said that would take a few weeks, but except for some nausea and weakness, she should manage it very well."

"You'll come with us?" she asked, amazed.

He glowered at her. "Of course I will," he said indignantly. "I'm part of the family. You said so."

She drew in a long, contented breath. She was tired and worried but she felt newborn. "You're the nicest man I've ever known," she said.

He cocked an eyebrow. "Nicer than the Army guy?"

She smiled. "Even nicer than Caleb."

He looked over her head and glowered even more. "Speak of the devil!"

A tall, dark-haired man in an Army uniform was striding down the hall toward them.

CHAPTER EIGHT

SASSY turned and, sure enough, Caleb was walking toward them in his Army uniform, complete with combat boots and beret. He looked very handsome.

"Caleb," Sassy said warmly, going to meet him. "How did you know we were here?"

He hugged her gently. "I have a cousin who works here. She remembered that I'd been down to see you in Hollister, and that your last name was Peale. How is your mother?"

"She just came out of surgery. Her prognosis is good. John found us a grant to pay for it all, isn't that incredible? I didn't know they had programs like that!"

Caleb knew they didn't. He looked at John and, despite the older man's foreboding expression, he smiled at him. He was quick enough to realize that John had intervened for Sassy's mother and didn't want anybody to know. "Yes, they do have grants, don't they? Nice of you to do that for them," he added, his dark eyes saying things to John that Sassy didn't see.

John relaxed a little. The boy might be competition, but his heart was in the right place. Sassy had said he was a friend, but Caleb here must care about her, to come right to the hospital when he knew about her mother. "They're a great bunch of people," he said simply.

"Yes, they are," Caleb agreed. He turned to smile down at Sassy while John fumed silently.

"Thank you for coming to see us," Sassy told the younger man.

"I wish I could stay," he told her, "but I'm on my way to the rimrocks right now. I'm due back at my assignment."

"The rimrocks?" Sassy asked, frowning.

"It's where the airport is," Caleb told her, grinning. "That's what we call it locally."

"I hope you have a safe flight back," she told him. "And a safe tour of duty."

"Now, that makes two of us," he agreed. "Don't forget to send me that photograph."

"I won't. So long, Caleb."

"So long." He bent and kissed her cheek, smiled ruefully at John, and walked back down the hall.

"What photograph?" John asked belligerently.

"It's not for him," she said, delighted that he looked jealous. "It's to throw his best friend off the track."

John was unconvinced. But just as he started to argue, the surgeon came into the waiting room, smiling wearily.

He shook hands with John and turned to Sassy. "Your mother is doing very well. She's in recovery right now, and then she'll go to the intensive care unit. Just for a couple of days," he added quickly when Sassy went pale and looked faint. "It's normal procedure. We want her watched day and night until she's stabilized."

"Can Selene and I see her?" Sassy asked. "And John?" she added, nodding to the man at her side.

The surgeon hesitated. "Have you ever seen anyone just out of surgery, young woman?" he asked gently.

"Well, there was Great-Uncle Jack, but I only got a glimpse of him . . . why?"

The surgeon looked apprehensive. "Post surgical patients are flour-white. They have tubes running out of them, they're connected to machines . . . it can be alarming if you aren't prepared for it."

"Mama's going to live, thanks to you," Sassy said, smiling. "She'll look beautiful. I don't mind the machines. They're helping her live. Right?"

The surgeon smiled back. Her optimism was contagious. "Right. I'll let you in to see her for five minutes, no longer," he said, "as soon as we move her into intensive care. It will be a little while," he added.

"We're not going anywhere," she replied easily.

He chuckled. "I'll send a nurse for you, when it's time."

"Thank you," Sassy said. "From the bottom of my heart."

The surgeon shifted. "It's what I do," he replied. "The most rewarding job in the world."

"I've never saved anybody's life, but I expect it would be a great job," she told him.

After he left, John gave her a wry look.

"I saved a man's life, once," he told her.

"You did? How?" she asked, waiting.

"I threw a baseball bat at him, and missed."

"Oh, you," she teased. She went close to him, wrapped her arms around him, and laid her head on his broad chest. "You're just wonderful."

His hand smoothed over her dark hair. Over her head, Selene was smiling at him with the same kind of happy, affectionate expression that he imagined was on Sassy's face. Despite the fear and apprehension of the ordeal, it was one of the best days of his life. He'd never felt so necessary.

• • •

Sassy was allowed into the intensive care unit just long enough to look at her mother and stand beside her. John was with her, the surgeon's whispered request getting him past the fiercely protective nurse in charge of the unit. Sassy was uneasy, despite her assurances, and she clung to John's hand as if she were afraid of falling without its warm support.

She stared at the still, white form in the hospital bed. Machines beeped. A breathing machine made odd noises as it pumped oxygen into Mrs. Peale's unconscious body. The shapeless, faded hospital gown was unfamiliar, like all the monitors and tubes that seemed to extrude from every inch of her mother's flesh. Mrs. Peale was white as a sheet. Her chest rose and fell very slowly. Her heartbeat was visible as the gown fluttered over her ample bosom.

"She's alive," John whispered. "She's going to get well and go home and be a different woman. You have to see the future, through the present."

Sassy looked up at him with tears in her eyes. "It's just . . . I love her so much."

He smiled tenderly and bent to kiss her forehead. "She loves you, too, honey. She's going to get well."

She drew in a shaky breath and got control of her emotions. She wiped at the tears. "Yes." She moved closer to the bed, bending over her mother.

She remembered that when she was a little girl she'd had a debilitating virus that had almost dehydrated her. Mrs. Peale had perched on her bed, feeding her ice chips around the clock to keep fluids in her. She'd fetched wet cloths and whispered that she loved Sassy, that everything was going to be all right. That loving touch had chased the fear and misery and sickness right out of the room. Mrs. Peale seemed to glow with it.

"It's going to be all right, Mama," she whispered, kissing the pale, cool brow. "We love you very much. We're going home, very soon."

Mrs. Peale didn't answer her, but her hand on its confining board jumped, almost imperceptibly.

John squeezed Sassy's hand. "Did you see that?" he asked, smiling. "She heard you."

Sassy squeezed back. "Of course she did."

Three days later, Mrs. Peale was propped up in bed eating Jell-O. She was weak and sore and still in a lot of pain, but she was smiling gamely.

"Didn't I tell you?" John chided Sassy. "She's too tough to let a little thing like major surgery get her down."

Mrs. Peale smiled at him. "You've been so kind to us, John," she said. Her voice was still a little hoarse from the breathing tubes, but she sounded cheerful just the same. "Sassy told me all about the palace you're keeping her and Selene in."

"Some palace," he chuckled. "It's just a place to

sleep." He stuck his hands into his jeans and his eyes twinkled. "But being kind goes with the job. I'm part of the family. She—" he pointed at Sassy "—said so."

"I did," Sassy confessed.

Mrs. Peale gave him a wry look. "But not too close a member . . . ?"

"Definitely not," he agreed at once, chuckling. He looked at Sassy in a way that made her blush. Then he compounded the embarrassment by laughing.

In the weeks that followed, John divided his time between Mrs. Peale's treatments in Billings and the growing responsibility for the new ranch that was just beginning to shape up. The barn was up, shiny and attractive with bricked aisles and spotless stalls with metal gates. The corral had white fences interlaced with hidden electrical fencing that complemented the cosmetic look of the wood. The pastures had been sowed with old prairie grasses, with which John was experimenting. The price of corn had gone through the roof, with the biofuel revolution. Ranchers were scrambling for new means of sustaining their herds, so native grasses were being utilized, along with concentrated pelleted feeds and vitamin supplements. John had also hired a nearby farmer to plant grains for him and keep them during the growing season. His contractor was building a huge new concrete feed silo to house the grains when they were harvested at the end of summer. It was a monumental job, getting the place renovated. John had delegated as much authority as he could, but there were still management decisions that had to be made by him.

Meanwhile, Bill Tarleton's trial went on the docket and pretrial investigations were going on by both the county district attorney and the public defender's office for the judicial circuit where Hollister was located. Sassy was interviewed by both sides. The questions made her very nervous and uneasy. The public defender seemed to think she'd enticed Mr. Tarleton to approach her in a sexual manner. It hurt her feelings.

She told John about it when he stopped by after supper one Friday evening to check on Mrs. Peale. He hadn't been into the feed store the entire week because of obligations out at the ranch.

"He'll make me sound like some cheap tart in court," she moaned. "It will make my mother and Selene look bad, too."

"Telling the truth won't make anyone look bad, dear," Mrs. Peale protested. She was sitting up in the living room knitting. A knitted cap covered her head. Her hair had already started to fall out from the radiation therapy she was receiving, but she hadn't let it get her down. She'd made a dozen caps in different colors and styles and seemed to be enjoying the project.

"You should listen to your mother," John agreed, smiling. "You don't want him to get away with it, Sassy. It wasn't your fault."

"That lawyer made it sound like it was. The assistant district attorney who questioned me asked what sort of clothes I wore to work, and I told him jeans and T-shirts, and not any low-cut ones, either. He smiled and said that it shouldn't have mattered if I'd worn a bikini. He said Mr. Tarleton had no business making me uncomfortable in my workplace, regardless of my clothing."

"I like that assistant district attorney," John said. "He's a firecracker. One day he'll end up in the state attorney general's office. They say he's got a perfect record of convictions in the two years he's prosecuted cases for this judicial circuit."

"I hope he makes Mr. Tarleton as uncomfortable as that public defender made me," Sassy said with feeling. She rubbed her bare arms, as if it chilled her, thinking about the trial. "I don't know how I'll manage, sitting in front of a jury and telling what happened."

"You just remember that the people in that jury will most likely be people who've known you all your life," Mrs. Peale interrupted.

"That's the other thing," Sassy sighed. "The D.A.'s victim assistance person said the defending attorney is trying to get the trial moved to Billings, on account of Mr. Tarleton can't get a fair trial here."

John frowned. That did put another face on things. But he'd testify, as would Sassy. Hopefully Tarleton would get what he deserved. John knew for a fact that if he hadn't intervened, it would have been much more than a minor assault. Sassy knew it, too.

"It was a bad day for Hollister when that man came to town," Mrs. Peale said curtly. "Sassy came home every day upset and miserable."

"You should have called the owner and complained," John told Sassy.

She grimaced. "I didn't dare. He didn't know me that well. I was afraid he'd think I was telling tales on Mr. Tarleton because I wanted his job."

"It's been done," John had to admit. "But you're not like that, Sassy. He'd have investigated and found that out."

She sighed. "It's water under the bridge now," she replied sadly. "I know it's the right thing to do, taking him to court. But what if he gets off and comes after me, or Mama or Selene for revenge?" she added, worried.

"If he does," John said, and his blue eyes glittered dangerously, "it will be the worst decision of his life. I promise you. As for getting off, if by some miracle he does, you'll file a civil suit against him for damages and I'll bankroll you."

"I knew you were a nice man from the first time I laid eyes on you," Mrs. Peale chuckled.

Sassy was smiling at him with her whole face.

She felt warm and protected and secure. She blushed when he looked back, with such an intent, piercing expression that her heart turned over.

"Why does life have to be so complicated?" Sassy asked after a minute.

John shrugged. "Beats me, honey," he said, getting to his feet and obviously unaware of the endearment that brought another soft blush to Sassy's face. "But it does seem to get more that way by the day." He checked his watch and grimaced. "I have to get back to the ranch. I've got an important call coming through. But I'll stop by tomorrow. We might take in a movie, if you're game."

Sassy grinned. "I'd love to." She looked at her mother and hesitated.

"I have a phone," her mother pointed out. "And Selene's here."

"You went out with the Army guy and didn't make a fuss," John muttered.

Mrs. Peale beamed. That was jealousy. Sassy seemed to realize it, too, because her eyes lit up.

"I'm not making a fuss," Sassy assured him. "And I love going to the movies."

John relented a little and grinned self-consciously. "Okay. I'll be along about six. That Chinese restaurant that just opened has good food—suppose I bring some along and we'll have supper before we go?"

They hesitated to accept. He'd done so much for them already . . .

"It's Chinese food, not precious jewels," he said. "Would you like to go out and look at my truck again? I make a handsome salary and I don't drink, smoke, gamble or run around with predatory women!"

Now Mrs. Peale and Sassy both looked sheepish and grinned.

"Okay," Sassy said. "But when I get rich and famous one day for my stock-clerking abilities, I'm paying you back for all of it."

He laughed. "That's a deal."

The Chinese food was a huge assortment of dishes, many of which could be stored in the refrigerator and provide meals for the weekend for the women and the child. They knew what he'd done, but they didn't complain again. He was bighearted and he wanted to help them. It seemed petty to argue.

After they ate, he helped Sassy up into the cab of the big pickup truck, got in himself, and drove off down the road. It was still light outside, but the sun was setting in brilliant colors. It was like a symphony of reds and oranges and yellows, against the silhouetted mountains in the distance.

"It's so beautiful here," Sassy said, watching the sunset. "I'd never want to live anyplace else."

He glanced at her. He was homesick for Medicine Ridge from time to time, but he liked Hollister, too. It was a small, homey place with nice people and plenty of wide-open country. The elbow room was delightful. You could drive for miles and not meet another car or even see a house.

"Are we going to the theater in town?" she asked John.

He grinned like a boy. "We are not," he told her. "I found a drive-in theater just outside the city limits. The owner started it up about a month ago. He said he'd gone to them when he was young and thought it was time to bring them back. I don't know that he'll be able to stay open long, but I thought we'd check it out, anyway."

"Wow," she exclaimed. "I've read about them in novels."

"Me, too, but I've never been to one. Our uncle used to talk about them."

"Is it in a town?" she asked.

"No. It's in the middle of a cowpasture. Cattle graze nearby."

She laughed delightedly. "You're watching a movie with the windows open and a cow sticks its head into the car with you," she guessed.

"I wouldn't be surprised."

"I like cows," she sighed. "I wouldn't mind."

"He runs beef cattle. Steers."

She looked at him. "Steers?"

"It's a bull with missing equipment," he told her, tongue-in-cheek.

"Then what's a cow?"

"It's a cow, if it's had calves. If it hasn't, it's a heifer."

"You know a lot about cattle."

"I've worked around them all my life," he said comfortably. "I love animals. We're going to have horses out at the ranch, too. You can come riding and bring Selene, any time you want."

"You'd have to teach Selene," she said. "She's never been on a horse and you'd have to coach me. It's been a long time since I've been riding."

He glanced at her with warm eyes. "I'd love that."

She laughed. "Me, too."

The drive-in was in a cleared pasture about a quarter of a mile off the main highway. There was a marquee, which listed the movie playing, this time a science-fiction one about a space freighter and its courageous crew which was fighting a technological empire that ran the inner planets of the solar system where it operated. They drove through a tree-lined dirt road down to the cleared pasture. There was room for about twenty cars, and six were already occupying one of three slight inclines that faced a huge blank screen. Each space had a pole, which contained two speakers, one for cars on either side of it. At the ticket stand, which was a drive-through affair manned by a teenager who looked like the owner John had already met, most likely his son, John paid for their tickets.

He pulled the truck up into an unoccupied space and cut off the engine, looking around amusedly.

"The only thing missing is a concession stand with drinks and pizza and a rest room," he mused. "Maybe he'll add that, later, if the drive-in catches on."

"It's nice out here, without all that," she mused, looking around.

"Yes, it is." He powered down both windows and brought the speaker in on his side of the truck. He turned up the volume just as the screen lit up with welcome messages and previews of coming attractions.

"This is great!" Sassy laughed.

"It is, isn't it?"

He tossed his hat into the small back seat of the double-cabbed truck, unfastened his seat belt, and stretched out. As an afterthought, he unfastened Sassy's belt and drew her into the space beside him, with his long arm behind her back and his cheek resting on her soft hair.

"Isn't that better?" he murmured, smiling.

One small hand went to press against his shirtfront as she curled closer with a sigh. "It's much better."

The first part of the movie was hilarious. But before it ended, they weren't watching anymore. John had looked down at Sassy's animated face in the flickering light from the movie screen and longing had grown in him like a hot tide. It had been a while since he'd felt Sassy's soft mouth under his lips and he was hungry for it. Since he'd known her, he hadn't had the slightest interest in other women. It was only Sassy.

He tugged on her hair so that she lifted her face to his. "Is this all you'll ever want, Sassy?" he asked gently. "Living in a small, rural town and working in a feed store? Will you miss knowing what it's like to go to college or work in a big city and meet sophisticated people?" he asked solemnly.

Her soft eyes searched his. "Why would I want to do that?" she asked with genuine interest.

"You're very young," he said grimly. "This is all you know."

"Mr. Barber, who runs the Ford dealership here, was born in Hollister and has never been outside the county in his whole life," she told him. "He's been married to Miss Jane since he was eighteen and she was sixteen. They have five sons."

He frowned. "Are you saying something?"

"I'm telling you that this is how people live here," she said simply. "We don't have extravagant tastes. We're country people. We're family. We get married. We have kids. We grow old watching our grandchildren grow up. Then we die. We're buried here. We have beautiful country where we can walk in the forest or ride through fields full of growing crops, or pass through pastures where cattle and horses graze. We have clear, unpolluted streams and blue skies. We sit on the porch after dark and listen to the crickets in the summer and watch lightning bugs flash green in the trees. If someone gets sick, neighbors come over to help. If someone dies, they bring food and comfort. Nobody in trouble is ever ignored. We have everything we need and want and love, right here in Hollister." She cocked her head. "What can a city offer us that would match that?"

He stared at her without speaking. He'd never heard it put exactly that way. He loved Medicine Ridge. But he'd been in college back East, and he'd traveled all over the world. He had choices. Sassy had never had the chance to make one. On the other hand, she sounded very mature as she recounted the reasons she was happy where she lived. There were people in John's acquaintance who'd never known who they were or where they belonged.

"What are you thinking?" she asked.

"That you're an old soul in a young body," he said.

She laughed. "My mother says that all the time."

"She's right. You have a profound grasp of life. So you're happy living here. What if you had a scholarship and you could go to college and study anything you liked?"

"Who'd take care of Mama and Selene?" she asked softly.

"Most women would be more interested in a career than being tied down to family responsibilities in this day and age."

"I've noticed," she sighed. "They interviewed this career woman on the news one night," she continued. "She'd moved to three different cities in a year, looking for a job where she felt fulfilled. She was divorced and had an eight-year-old son. I wonder how he enjoyed being in three different schools in one year so that she could feel fulfilled?"

He frowned. "Kids adjust."

"Of course they do," she replied. "Mostly they adjust to having one parent, because so many people divorce, or they adjust to being suddenly part of somebody else's family. They adjust to parents who work all the time and are too tired to play or talk to them after school. They're encouraged to participate in all sorts of after-school activities as well, so they have baseball and football and soccer and band and theater and all those time-consuming responsibilities when they're not studying." She settled closer to John. "So exactly when do parents have time to get to know their kids? Everybody's so busy these days. I've read that some kids have to text-message their parents and make appointments to meet. And they wonder why kids are so screwed up."

He sighed. "I guess my brother and I were protected from a lot of that. Our uncle kept us close on the ranch. We played sports, but we were confined to one, and we had chores every day that had to be done. We didn't have cell phones or cars, and we mostly stayed at home until he thought we were old enough to drive. We always ate together and most nights we played board games or went outside with the telescopes to learn about the stars. He wasn't big on school activities, either. He said they were a corrupting influence, because we had city kids in our school with what he called outrageous ideas of morality."

She laughed. "That's what Mama called some of the kids at my school." She grimaced. "I guess I've been very sheltered. I do have a cell phone, but I don't know how to do text-messages."

"I'll teach you," he told her, smiling. "I do it a lot."

"I guess your phone does stuff besides just making calls."

"I have the Internet, movies, music, sports, and e-mail on mine," he told her.

"Wow. Mine just gets phone calls."

He laughed. She was so out of touch. But he loved her that way. The smile faded as he looked down into her soft, melting eyes. He dropped his gaze to her mouth, faintly pink, barely parted.

"I suppose the future doesn't come with guarantees," he said to himself. He bent slowly. "I've been sitting here for five minutes remembering how your soft lips felt under my mouth, Sassy," he whispered as his parted lips met hers. "I ache like a boy for you."

As he spoke, he drew her across the seat, across

his lap, and kissed her with slow, building hunger. His big hand deftly moved buttons out of buttonholes and slid right inside her bra with a mastery that left her breathless and too excited to protest.

He caressed the hard tip with slow, teasing movements while he fed on her mouth, teasing it, too, with slow, brief contacts that eventually made her moan and arch up toward him.

Her skin felt hot. She ached to have him take off her blouse and everything under it and look at her. She wanted to feel his lips swallowing that hard-tipped softness. It was madness. She could hear her own heartbeat, feel the growing desire that built inside her untried body. She'd never wanted a man before. Now she wanted him with a reckless abandon that blasted every sane reason for protest right out of her melting body.

John lifted his head, frustrated, and glanced around him in the darkness. The scene on the screen was subdued and so was the lighting. Nobody could see them. He bent his head again and, unobtrusively, suddenly stripped Sassy's blouse and bra up to her chin. His blazing eyes found her breasts, adored them. He shivered with need.

She arched faintly, encouraging him. He bent to her breasts and slowly drew one of them right inside his mouth, pulling at it gently as his tongue explored the hardness and drew a harsh moan from her lips.

The sound galvanized him. His mouth became rough. The arm behind her was like steel. His free hand slid down her bare belly and right into the opening of her jeans. He was so aroused that he didn't even realize where they were.

At least, he didn't realize it until something wet and rubbery slid over his bent head through the passenger window.

It took him a minute to realize it wasn't, couldn't be, Sassy's mouth. It was very wet. He forced his own head up and looked toward Sassy's window. A very large bovine head was inside the open window of the truck. It was licking him.

CHAPTER NINE

"SASSY?" he asked, his voice hoarse with lingering passion.

She opened her eyes. "What?"

"Look out your window."

She turned her head and met the steer's eyes. "Aaaah!" she exclaimed.

He burst out laughing. He smoothed down her blouse and bra and sat up, his hand going gingerly to his hair. "Good Lord! I wondered why my hair felt so wet."

She fumbled her bra back on, embarrassed and amused at the same time. The little steer had moved back from the window, but it was still curious. It let out a loud "MOOOO." Muffled laughter came from a nearby car.

"Well, so much for my great idea that this was a good place to make out," John chuckled, straightening his shirt with a sigh. "I guess it wasn't a bad thing to get interrupted," he added, with a rueful smile at Sassy's red face. "Things were getting a little intense."

He didn't seem to be embarrassed at all, but Sassy had never gone so far with a man before and she felt fragile. She was uneasy that she hadn't denied him such intimate access to her body. And she couldn't forget where his other hand had been moving when the steer came along.

"Don't," John said softly when he read her expression. His fingers caught hers and linked into them. "It was perfectly natural."

"I guess you . . . do that all the time," she stammered.

He shrugged. "I used to. But since I met you, I haven't wanted to do it with anyone else."

If it was a line, it sounded sincere. She looked at him with growing hope. "Really?"

His fingers tightened on hers. "We've been through a lot of intense situations together in a little bit of time. Tarleton's assault. Your mother's close call. The cancer treatments." He looked into her eyes. "You said that I was like part of your family and that's how I feel, too. I'm at home when I'm with you." He looked down at their linked hands. “I want it to go on,” he said hesitantly. “I want us to be together. I want you in my life from now on.” He drew in a long breath. “I ache to have you.”

She was uncomfortable with the way he said it, not understanding that he’d never tried to make a commitment to another woman in his life; not even when he was intimate with other women.

“You want to sleep with me,” she said bluntly.

He smoothed his thumb over her cold fingers. “I want to do everything with you,” he replied. “You’re too young,” he added quietly. “But, then, my brother just married a woman ten years his junior and they’re ecstatically happy. It can work. I guess it depends on the woman, and we’ve already agreed that you’re mature for your age.”

“You aren’t exactly over the hill, John,” she replied, still curious about what he was suggesting. “And you’re very attractive.” She gave him a gamine look. “Even small hoofed animals are drawn to you.”

He glared at her.

“Don’t look at me,” she laughed. “It was you that the little steer was kissing.”

He touched his wet hair and winced. “God knows where his mouth has been.”

She laughed again. “Well, at least he has good taste.”

“Thanks. I think.” He pulled a red work rag from the console and dried his hair where the steer had licked it. He was watching Sassy. "You don't understand what I'm saying, do you?"

"Not really," she confessed.

"I suppose I'm making a hash of it," he muttered. "But I've never done this before."

"Asked someone to live with you, you mean," she said haltingly.

He met her eyes evenly. "Asked someone to marry me, Sassy."

She just stared. For a minute, she wasn't sure she wasn't dreaming. But his gaze was intent, intimate. He was waiting.

She let out the breath she'd been holding. She started to speak and then stopped, confused. "I . . ."

"If you've noticed any bad habits that disturb you, I'll try to change them," he mused, smiling, because she wasn't refusing.

"Oh, no, it's not that. I . . . I have a lot of baggage," she began nervously.

Then he remembered what she told him some time back, that her infrequent dates had said they didn't want to get involved with a woman who had so much responsibility for her family.

He grinned. "I love your baggage," he said. "Your mother and adopted sister are like part of my family already." He shrugged. "So I'll have more dependents." He gave her a wicked look. "Income tax time won't be so threatening."

She laughed out loud. He wasn't intimidated. He didn't mind. She threw her arms around him and kissed him so fervently that he forgot what they'd been talking about and just kissed her back until they had to come up for air.

"But I'll still work," she promised breathlessly, her eyes sparkling like fireworks. "I'm not going to sit down and make you support all three of us, I'll carry my part of the load!" She laughed, unaware of his sudden stillness, of the guilty look on his face. "It will be fun, making our way together. Hard times are what bring people close, you know, even more than the good times."

"Sassy, there are some things we're going to have to talk about," he said slowly.

"A lot of things," she agreed dreamily, laying her cheek against his broad, warm chest. "I never dreamed you might want to marry me. I'll try to be the best wife in the world. I'll cook and clean and work my fingers to the bone. I like horses and cattle. I'll help you with chores on the ranch, too."

She was cutting his heart open and she didn't know it. He'd lied to her. He hadn't thought of the consequences. He should have been honest with her from the beginning. But he realized then that she'd never have come near him if he'd walked into that feed store in his real persona. The young woman who worshipped the lowly cattle foreman would draw back and stand in awe of the wealthy cattle baron who could walk into a store and buy anything he fancied without even looking at a price tag. It was a sickening thought. She was going to feel betrayed, at best. At worst, she might think he was playing some game with her.

He smoothed his hand over her soft hair. "Well, it can wait another day," he murmured as he kissed her forehead. "There's plenty of time for serious discussions." He tilted her mouth up to his. "Tonight, we're just engaged and celebrating. Come here."

By the time they got back to her house, they were both disheveled and their mouths were swollen. Sassy had never been so happy in her life.

John had consoled himself that he still had time to tell Sassy the truth. He had no way of knowing that Bill Tarleton and his attorney had just gone before the district circuit judge in the courthouse in Billings for a hearing on a motion to dismiss all charges against him. The reason behind the motion, the attorney stated, was that the eyewitness who was to testify against Tarleton was romantically involved with the so-called victim and was, in fact, no common cowboy, but a wealthy cattleman from Medicine Ridge. The defense argued that this new information changed the nature of the accusation from a crime to an act of jealousy. It was a rich man victimizing a poor man because he was jealous of the man's attentions to his girlfriend.

The state attorney, who was also present at the hearing, argued that the new information made no difference to the primary charge, which was one of sexual assault and battery. A local doctor would testify to the young lady's physical condition after the assault. The public defender argued that he'd seen the doctor's report and it only mentioned reddish marks and bruising, on the young lady's arms, nothing more. That could not be construed as injury sustained in the course of a sexual assault, so only the alleged assault charge was even remotely applicable.

The judge took the case under advisement and promised a decision within the week. Meanwhile, the assistant district attorney handling the case in circuit court, showed up at Sassy's home the following Monday evening soon after Sassy had put Selene to bed to discuss the case. His name was James Addy.

"Mr. Tarleton is alleging that Mr. Callister inflated the charges out of jealousy because of the attention Mr. Tarleton was paying you," Addy said in a businesslike tone, opening his briefcase on the dining room table while Sassy sat gaping at him.

"Mr. Callister? Who is that?" she asked, confused. "John Taggert rescued me. Mr. Tarleton kissed me and was trying to force me down on the floor. I screamed for help and Mr. Taggert, who came into the store at that moment, came to my assistance. I don't know any Mr. Callister."

The attorney stared at her. "You don't know who John Callister is?" he asked, aghast. "He and his brother Gil own the Medicine Ridge Ranch. It's world famous as a breeding bull enterprise. Aside from that, they have massive land holdings not only in Montana, but in adjoining states, including real estate and mining interests. Their parents own the Sportsman Enterprises chain of magazines. The family is one of the wealthiest in the country."

"Yes," Sassy said, trying to wrap her mind around the strange monolog, "I've heard of them. But what do they have to do with John Taggert, except that they're his bosses?" she asked innocently.

The attorney finally got it. She didn't know who her suitor actually was. A glance around the room was enough to tell him her financial status. It was unlikely that a millionaire would be seriously interested in such a poor woman. Apparently Callister had been playing some game with her. He frowned. It was a cruel game.

"The man's full name is John Taggert Callister," he said in a gentler tone. "He's Gil Callister's younger brother."

Sassy's face lost color. She'd been dreaming of a shared life with John, of working to build something good together, along with her family. He was a millionaire. That sort of man moved in high society, had money to burn. He was up here overhauling a new ranch for the conglomerate. Sassy had been handy and she amused him, so he was playing with her. It hadn't been serious, not even when he asked her to marry him! She felt sick to her stomach. She didn't know what to do now. And how was she going to tell her mother and Selene the truth?

She folded her arms around her chest and sat like a stone, her green eyes staring at the attorney, pleading with him to tell her it was all a lie, a joke.

He couldn't. He grimaced. "I'm very sorry," he said genuinely. "I thought you knew the truth."

"Not until now," she said in a subdued tone. She closed her eyes. The pain was lancing, enveloping. Her life was falling apart around her.

He drew in a long breath, searching for the right words. "Miss Peale, I hate to have to ask you this. But was there an actual assault?"

She blinked. What had he asked? She met his eyes. "Mr. Tarleton kissed me and tried to handle me and I resisted him. He was angry. He got a hard grip on me and was trying to force me down on the floor when Mr. Taggert—" She stopped and swallowed, hard. "Mr. Callister, that is, came to help me. He pulled Mr. Tarleton off me. Then he called law enforcement."

The lawyer was looking worried. "You were taken to a doctor. What were his findings?"

"Well, I had some bruises and I was sore. He ripped my blouse. I guess there wasn't a lot of physical evidence. But it did scare me. I was upset and crying."

"Miss Peale, was there an actual *sexual* assault?"

She began to understand what he meant. “Oh! Well . . . no,” she stammered. “He kissed me and he tried to fondle me, but he didn’t try to take any of my other clothes off, if that’s what you mean.”

“That’s what I mean.” He sat back in his chair. “We can’t prosecute for sexual assault and battery on the basis of an unwanted kiss. We can charge him with sexual assault for any sexual contact which is unwanted. However, the law provides that if he’s convicted, the maximum sentence is six months in jail or a fine not to exceed $500. If in the course of sexual contact the perpetrator inflicts bodily injury, he can get from four years to life in prison. In this case, however, you would be required to show that injury resulted from the attempted kiss. Quite frankly,” he added, “I don’t think a jury, even under the circumstances, would consider unwanted touching and bruising to be worth giving a man a life sentence.”

She sighed. “Yes. It does seem a bit drastic, even to me. Is it true that he doesn’t have any prior convictions?” she asked curiously.

He shook his head. “We found out that he was arrested on a sexual harassment charge in another city, but he was cleared, so there was no conviction.”

She was tired of the whole thing. Tired of remembering Tarleton’s unwanted advances, tired of being tied to the memory as long as the court case dragged on. If she insisted on prosecuting him for an attack, she couldn't produce any real proof. His attorney would take her apart on the witness stand, and she'd be humiliated yet again.

But as bad as that thought was, it was worse to think about going into court and asking them to put a man, even Tarleton, in prison for the rest of his life because he'd tried to kiss her. The lawyer was right. Tarleton might have intended a sexual assault, but all he managed was a kiss and some bruising. That was uncomfortable, and disgusting, but hardly a major crime. Still, she hated letting him get off so lightly.

She almost protested. It had been a little more than bruising. The man had intended much more, and he'd done it to some other poor girl who'd been too shamed to force him to go to trial. Sassy had guts. She could do this.

But then she had a sudden, frightening thought. If John Taggert Callister was called to appear for the prosecution, she realized suddenly, it would become a media event. He was famous. His presence at the trial would draw the media. There would be news crews, cameras, reporters. There might even be national exposure. Her mother would suffer for it. So would Selene. For herself, she would have taken the chance. For her mother, still undergoing cancer treatments and unsuited to stress of any kind right now, she could not.

Her shoulders lifted. "Mr. Addy, the trial will come with a media blitz if Mr . . . Mr. Callister is called to testify for me, won't it? My mother and Selene could be talked about on those horrible entertainment news programs if it came out that I was poor and John was rich and there was an attempted sexual assault in the mix. Think how twisted they could make it sound. It would be the sort of sordid subject some people in the news media love to get their hands on these days. Just John's name would guarantee that people would be interested in what happened. They could make a circus out of it."

He hesitated. "That shouldn't be a consideration . . ."

"My mother has lung cancer," she replied starkly. "She's just been through major surgery and is now undergoing radiation and chemo for it. She can't take any more stress than she's already got. If there's even a chance that this trial could bring that sort of publicity, I can't take it. So what can I do?"

Mr. Addy considered the question. "I think we can plea bargain him to a charge of sexual assault with the lighter sentence. I know, it's not perfect," he told her. "He'd likely get the fine and some jail time, even if he gets probation. And it would at least go on the record as a conviction and any future transgression on his part would land him in very hot water. He has a public defender, but he seems anxious to avoid spending a long time in jail waiting for the trial. I think he'll agree to the lesser charge. Especially considering who the witness is. When he has time to think about the consequences of trying to drag John Callister's good name through the mud, and consider what sort of attorneys the Callisters would produce for a trial, I believe he'll jump at the plea bargain."

She considered that, and then the trauma of a jury trial with all the media present. This way, at least Tarleton would now have a criminal record, and it might be enough to deter him from any future assaults on other women. "Okay," she said. "As long as he doesn't get away with it."

"Oh, he won't get away with it, Miss Peale," he said solemnly. "I promise you that." He pondered for a minute. "However, if you'd rather stand firm on the original charge, I'll prosecute him, despite the obstacles. Is this plea bargain what you really want?"

She sighed sadly. "Not really. I'd love to hang him out to dry. But I have to consider my mother. It's the only possible way to make him pay for what he tried to do without hurting my family. If it goes to a jury trial, even with the media all around, he might walk away a free man because of the publicity. You said they were already trying to twist it so that it looks like John was just jealous and making a fuss because he could, because he was rich and powerful. I know the Callisters can afford the best attorneys, but it wouldn't be right to put them in that situation, either. Mr. Callister has two little nieces . . ." She grimaced. "You know, the legal system isn't altogether fair sometimes."

He smiled. "I agree. But it's still the best system on earth," he replied.

"I hope I'm doing the right thing," she said on a sigh. "If he gets out and hurts some other woman because I backed down, I'll never get over it."

He gave her a long look. "You aren't backing down, Miss Peale. You're compromising. It may look as if he's getting away with it. But he isn't."

She liked him. She smiled. "Okay, then."

He closed his briefcase and got to his feet. He held out his hand and shook hers. "He'll have a criminal record," he promised her. "If he ever tries to do it again, in Montana, I can promise you that he'll spend a lot of time looking at the world through vertical bars." He meant every word.

"Thanks, Mr. Addy."

"I'll let you know how things work out. Good evening."

Sassy watched him go with quiet, thoughtful eyes. She was compromising on the case, but on behalf of a good cause. She couldn't put her mother through the nightmare of a trial and the vicious publicity it would bring on them. Mrs. Peale had suffered enough.

She went back into the house. Mrs. Peale was coming out of the bedroom, wrapped in her chenille housecoat, pale and weak. "Could you get me some pineapple juice, sweetheart?" she asked, forcing a smile.

"Of course!" Sassy ran to get it. "Are you all right?" she asked worriedly.

"Just a little sick. That's nothing to worry about, it goes with the treatments. At least I'm through with them for a few weeks." She frowned. "What's wrong? And who was that man you were talking to?"

"Here, back to bed." Sassy went with her, helping her down on the bed and tucking her under the covers with her glass of cold juice. She sat down beside her. "That was the assistant district attorney—or one of them, anyway. A Mr. Addy. He came to talk to me about Mr. Tarleton. He wants to offer him a plea bargain so we don't end up in a messy court case."

Mrs. Peale frowned. "He's guilty of harassing you. He assaulted you. He should pay for it."

"He will. There's jail time and a fine for it," she replied, candy-coating her answer. "He'll have a criminal record. But I won't have to be grilled and humiliated by his attorney on the stand."

Mrs. Peale sipped her juice. She thought about what a trial would be like for Sassy. She'd seen such trials on her soap operas. She sighed. "All right, dear. If you're satisfied, I am, too." She smiled. "Have you heard from John? He was going to bring me some special chocolates when he came back."

Sassy hesitated. She couldn't tell her mother. Not yet. "I haven't heard from him," she said.

"You don't look well . . ."

"I'm just fine," Sassy said, grinning. "Now you go back to bed. I'm going to reconcile the bank statement and get Selene's clothes ready for school tomorrow."

"All right, dear." She settled back into the pillows. "You're too good to me, Sassy," she added. "Once I get back on my feet, I want you to go a lot of places with John. I'm going to be fine, thanks to him and those doctors in Billings. I can take care of myself and Selene, finally, and you can have a life of your own."

"You stop that," Sassy chided. "I love you. Nothing I do for you, or Selene, is a chore."

"Yes, but you've had a ready-made family up until now," Mrs. Peale said softly. "It's limited your social life."

"My social life is just dandy, thanks."

The older woman grinned. "I'll say! Wait until John gets back. He's got a surprise waiting for you."

"Has he, really?" Sassy wondered if it was the surprise the attorney had just shared with her. She was too sick to care, but she couldn't let on. Her mother was so happy. It would be cruel to dash all her hopes and reveal the truth about the young man Mrs. Peale idolized.

"He has! Don't you stay up too late. You're looking peaked, dear."

"I'm just tired. We've been putting up tons of stock in the feed store," she lied. She smiled. "Good night, Mama."

"Good night, dear. Sleep well."

As if, Sassy thought as she closed the door. She gave up on paperwork a few minutes later and went to bed. She cried herself to sleep.

John walked into the feed store a day later, back from an unwanted but urgent business trip to Colorado. He spotted Sassy at the counter and walked up to it with a beaming smile.

She looked up and saw him, and he knew it was all over by the expression on her face. She was apprehensive, uncomfortable. She fidgeted and could barely meet his intent gaze.

He didn't even bother with preliminary questions. His eyes narrowed angrily. "Who told you?" he asked tersely.

She drew in a breath. He looked scary like that. Now that she knew who he really was, knew the power and fame behind his name, she was intimidated. This man could write his own ticket. He could go anywhere, buy anything, do anything he liked. He was worlds away from Sassy, who lived in a house with a leaky roof. He was like a stranger. The smiling, easygoing cowboy she thought he was had become somebody totally different.

"It was the assistant district attorney," she said in

a faint tone. "He came to see me. Mr. Tarleton was going to insinuate that you were jealous of him and forced me to file a complaint . . ."

He exploded. "I'll get attorneys in here who will put him away for the rest of his miserable life," he said tersely. He looked as if he could do that single-handed.

"No!" She swallowed. "No. Please. Think what it would do to Mama if a whole bunch of reporters came here to cover the story because of . . . because of who you are," she pleaded. "Stress makes everything so much worse for her."

He looked at her intently. "I hadn't thought about that," he said quietly. "I'm sorry."

"Mr. Addy says that Mr. Tarleton will probably agree to plead guilty or no contest to the sexual assault charge." She sighed. "There's a fine and jail time. He was willing to prosecute on the harder charge, but there would have to be proof that he did more than just kiss me and handle me . . ."

He frowned. He knew what she meant. A jury would be unlikely to convict for sexual assault and battery on an unwanted kiss and some groping, and how could they prove that Tarleton had intended much more? It made him angry. He wanted the man to go to prison. But Mrs. Peale would pay the price. In her delicate condition, it would probably kill her to have to watch Sassy go through the trial, even if she didn't get to court. John's name would guarantee news interest. Just the same, he was going to have a word with Mr. Addy. Sassy never had to know.

"How is your mother?" he asked.

"She's doing very well," she replied, her tone a little stilted. He did intimidate her now. "The treatments have left her a little anemic and weak, and there's some nausea, but they gave her medicine for that." She didn't add that it was bankrupting her to pay for it. She'd already had to pawn her grandfather's watch and pistol to manage a month's worth. She wasn't admitting that.

"I brought her some chocolates," he told her. He smiled gently. "She likes the Dutch ones."

She was staring at him with wide, curious eyes. "You'll spoil her," she replied.

He shrugged. "So? I'm rich. I can spoil people if I want to."

"Yes, I know, but . . ."

"If you were rich, and I wasn't," he replied solemnly, "would you hesitate to do anything you could for me, if I was in trouble?"

"Of course not," she assured him.

"Then why should it bother you if I spoil your mother a little? Especially, now, when she's had so much illness."

"It doesn't, really. It's just—" She stopped dead. The color went out of her face as she stared at him and suddenly realized how much he'd done for them.

"What's wrong?" he asked.

"There was no grant to pay for that surgery, and the treatments," she said in a choked tone. "You paid for it! You paid for it all!"

CHAPTER TEN

JOHN grimaced. "Sassy, there was no other way," he said, trying to reason with her. She looked anguished. "Your mother would have died. I checked your company insurance coverage when I had Buck put you on the payroll as assistant manager. It didn't have a major medical option. I told Buck to shop around for a better plan, but your mother's condition went critical before we could find one."

She knew her heart was going to beat her to death. She'd never be able to pay him back, not even the interest on the money he'd spent on her mother. She'd been poor all her life, but she'd never felt it like this. It had never hurt so much.

"You're part of my life now," he said softly. "You and your mother and Selene. Of course I was going to do all I could for you. For God's sake, don't try to reduce what we feel for each other to dollars and cents!"

"I can't pay you back," she groaned.

"Have I asked you to?" he returned.

"But . . ." she protested, ready for a long battle.

The door opened behind them and Theodore

Graves, the police chief walked in. His lean face was set in hard lines. He nodded at John and approached Sassy.

He pushed his Stetson back over jet-black hair. "That assistant district attorney, Addy, said you agreed to let Tarleton plea bargain to a lesser charge," he said. "He won't discuss the case with me and I can't intimidate him the way I intimidate most people. So I'd like to know why."

She sighed. He made her feel guilty. "It's Mama," she told him. "He—" she indicated John "—is very well-known. If it goes to court, reporters will show up to find out why he's mixed up in a sexual assault case. Mama will get stressed out, the cancer will come back, and we'll bury her."

Graves grimaced. "I hadn't thought about that. About the stress, I mean." He frowned. "What do you mean, he's well-known?" he added, indicating John. "He's a ranch foreman."

"He's not," Sassy said with a long sigh. "He's John Callister."

Graves lifted a thick, dark eyebrow. "Of the Callister ranching empire over in Medicine Ridge?"

John lifted a shoulder. "Afraid so."

"Oh, boy."

"Listen, at least he'll have a police record," Sassy said stubbornly. "Think about it. Do you really want a media circus right here in Hollister?

Mr. Tarleton would probably love it," she added miserably.

"He probably would," Graves had to agree. He stuck his hands into his slacks pockets. "Seventy-five years ago, we'd have turned him out into the woods and sent men with guns after him."

"Civilized men don't do things like that," Sassy reminded him. "Especially policemen."

Graves shrugged. "So sue me. I never claimed to be civilized. I'm a throwback." He drew in a long breath. "All right, as long as the polecat gets some serious time in the slammer, I can be generous and put up the rope I just bought."

Sassy wondered how the chief thought Tarleton would get a jail sentence when Mr. Addy had hinted that Tarleton would probably get probation.

"Good of you," John mused.

"Pity he didn't try to escape when we took him up to Billings for the motion hearing," Graves said thoughtfully. "I volunteered to go along with the deputy sheriff who transported him. I even wore my biggest caliber revolver, special, just in case." He pursed his lips and brightened. "Somebody might leave a door open, in the detention center . . ."

"Don't you dare," John said firmly. "You're not the only one who's disappointed. I was looking forward to the idea of having him spend the next fifteen years or so with one of the inmates who has the most cigarettes. But I'm not willing to see my future mother-in-law die over it."

"Mother-in-law?" Graves gave him a wry look from liquid black eyes in a lean, tanned face.

Sassy blushed. "Now, we have to talk about that," she protested.

"We already did," John said. "You promised to marry me."

"That was before I knew who you were," she shot back belligerently.

He grinned. "That's more like it," he mused. "The deference was wearing a little thin," he explained.

She flushed even more. She had been behaving like a working girl with the boss, instead of an equal. She shifted. She was still uncomfortable thinking about his background and comparing it to her own.

"I like weddings," Graves commented.

John glanced at him. "You do?"

He nodded. "I haven't been to one in years, of course, and I don't own a good suit anymore." He shrugged. "I guess I could buy one, if I got invited to a wedding."

John burst out laughing. "You can come to ours. I'll make sure you get an invitation."

Graves smiled. "That's a deal." He glanced at Sassy, who still looked undecided. "If I lived in a house that looked like yours, and drove a piece of scrap metal like that vehicle you ride around in, I'd say yes when a financially secure man asked me to marry him."

Sassy almost burst trying not to laugh. “Has any financially secure man asked you to marry him lately, Chief?”

He glared at her. “I was making a point.”

“Several of them,” Sassy returned. “But I do appreciate your interest. I wouldn’t mind sending Mr. Tarleton to prison myself, if the cost wasn’t so high.”

He pursed his lips and his black eyes twinkled. “Now that’s a coincidence. I’ve thought about nothing else except sending Mr. Tarleton to prison for the past few weeks. In fact, it never hurts to recommend a prison to the district attorney,” he said pleasantly. “I know one where even the chaplain has to carry a Taser.”

“Mr. Addy already said he isn’t likely to get jail time, since he’s a first offender,” Sassy said sadly.

“Now isn’t that odd,” the chief replied with a wicked grin. “I spent some quality time on the computer yesterday and I turned up a prior conviction for sexual assault over in Wyoming, where Mr. Tarleton was working two years ago. He got probation for that one. Which makes him a repeat offender.” He looked almost angelic. “I just told Addy. He was almost dancing in the street.”

Sassy gasped. “Really?”

He chuckled. “I thought you’d like hearing that. I figured that a man with his attitude had to have a conviction somewhere. He didn’t have one in Montana, so I started looking in surrounding states. I checked the criminal records in Wyoming, got a hit, and called the district attorney in the court circuit where it was filed. What a story I got from him! So I took it straight to Addy this morning." He gave her a wry look. "But I did want to know why you let him plead down, and Addy wouldn't tell me."

"Now I feel better, about agreeing to the plea bargain," Sassy said. "His record will affect the sentence, won't it?"

"It will, indeed," Graves assured her. "In another interesting bit of irony, the judge hearing his case had to step down on account of a family emergency. The new judge in his case is famous for her stance on sexual assault cases." He leaned forward. "She's a woman."

Sassy's eyes lit up. "Poor Mr. Tarleton."

"Right." John chuckled. "Good of you to bring us the latest news."

Graves smiled at him. "I thought it would be a nice surprise." He glanced at Sassy. "I understand now why you made the decision you did. Your mom's a sweet lady. It's like a miracle that the surgery saved her."

"Yes," Sassy agreed. Her eyes met John's. "It is a miracle."

Graves pulled his wide-brimmed hat low over his eyes. "Don't forget that wedding invitation," he reminded John. "I'll even polish my good boots."

"I won't forget," John assured him.

"Thanks again," she told the chief.

He smiled at her. "I like happy endings."

When he was gone, John turned back to Sassy with a searching glance. "I'm coming to get you after supper," he informed her. "We've got a lot to talk about."

"John, I'm poor," she began.

He leaned across the counter and kissed her warmly. "I'll be poor, if I don't have you," he said softly. He pulled a velvet-covered box out of his pocket and put it in her hands. "Open that after I leave."

"What is it?" she asked dimly.

"Something for us to talk about, of course." He winked at her and smiled broadly. He walked out the door and closed it gently behind him.

Sassy opened the box. It was a gold wedding band with an embossed vine running around it. There was a beautiful diamond ring that was its companion. She stared at them until tears burned her eyes. A man bought a set of rings like this when he meant them to be heirlooms, handed down from generation to generation. She clutched it close to her heart. Despite the differences, she knew what she was going to say.

It took Mrs. Peale several minutes to understand what Sassy was telling her.

"No, dear," she insisted. "John *works* for Mr. Callister. That's what he told us."

"Yes, he did, but he didn't mention that Taggert was his middle name, not his last name," Sassy replied patiently. "He and his brother, Gil, own one of the most famous ranches in the West. Their parents own that sports magazine Daddy always used to read before he left."

The older woman sat back with a rough sigh. "Then what was he doing coming around here?" she asked, and looked hurt.

"Well, that's the interesting part," Sassy replied, blushing. "It seems that he . . . well, he wants to . . . that is . . ." She jerked out the ring box, opened it, and put it in her mother's hands. "He brought that to me this morning."

Mrs. Peale eyed the rings with fascination. "How beautiful," she said softly. She touched the pattern on the wedding band. "He means these to be heirlooms, doesn't he? I had your grandmother's wedding band," she added sadly, "but I had to sell it when you were little and we didn't have the money for a doctor when you got sick." She looked up at her daughter with misty eyes. "He's really serious, isn't he?"

"Yes, I think he is," Sassy sighed. She sat down next to her mother. "I still can't believe it."

"That hospital bill," Mrs. Peale began slowly. "There was no grant, was there?"

Sassy shook her head. "John said that he couldn't stand by and let you die. He's fond of you."

"I'm fond of him, too," she replied. "And he wants to marry my daughter." Her eyes suddenly had a faraway look. "Isn't it funny? Remember what I told you my grandmother said to me, that I'd be poor but my daughter would live like royalty?" She laughed. "My goodness!"

"Maybe she really did know things." Sassy took the rings from her mother's hand and stared at them. It did seem that dreams came true.

John came for her just at sunset. He took time to kiss Mrs. Peale and Selene and assure them that he wasn't taking Sassy out of the county when they married.

"I'm running this ranch myself," he assured her with a warm smile. "Sassy and I will live here. The house has plenty of room, so you two can move in with us."

Mrs. Peale looked worried. "John, it may not look like much, but I was born in this house. I've lived in it all my life, even after I married."

He bent and kissed her again. "Okay. If you want to stay here, we'll do some fixing up and get you a companion. You can choose her."

Her old eyes brightened. "You'd do that for me?" she exclaimed.

"Nothing is too good for my second mama," he assured her, and he wasn't joking. "Now Sassy and I are going out to talk about all the details. We'll be back later."

She kissed him back. "You're going to be the nicest son-in-law in the whole world."

"You'd better believe it," he replied.

John took her over to the new ranch, where the barn was up, the stable almost finished, and the house completely remodeled. He walked her through the kitchen and smiled at her enthusiasm.

"We can have a cook, if you'd rather," he told her.

She looked back at him, running her hand lovingly over a brand-new stove with all sorts of functions. "Oh, I'd love to work in here myself." She hesitated. "John, about Mama and Selene . . ."

He moved away from the doorjamb he'd been leaning against and pulled her into his arms. His expression was very serious. "I know you're worried about her. But I was serious about the companion. It's just that she needs to be a nurse. We won't tell your mother that part of it just yet."

"She's not completely well yet. I know a nurse will look out for her, but . . ."

He smiled. "I like the way you care about people," he said softly. "I know she's not able to stay by herself and she won't admit it. But we're close enough that you can go over there every day and check on her."

She smiled. "Okay. I just worry."

"That's one of the things I most admire about you," he told her. "That big heart."

"You have to travel a lot, to show cattle, don't you?" she asked, recalling something she'd read in a magazine about the Callisters, before she knew who John was.

"I used to," he said. "We have a cattle foreman at the headquarters ranch in Medicine Ridge who's showing Gil's bulls now. I'll put on one here to do the same for us. I don't want to be away from home unless I have to, now."

She beamed. "I don't want you away from home, unless I can go with you."

He chuckled. "Two minds running in the same direction." He shifted his weight a little. "I didn't tell your mother, but I've already interviewed several women who might want the live-in position. I had their backgrounds checked as well," he added, chuckling. "When I knew I was going to marry you, I started thinking about how your mother would cope without you."

"You're just full of surprises," she said, breathless.

He grinned. "Yes, I am. The prospective housemates will start knocking on the door about ten Friday morning. You can tell her when we get home." He sobered. "She'll be happier in her own home, Sassy. Uprooting her will be as traumatic as the chemo was. You can visit her every day and twice on Sundays. I'll come along, too."

"I think you're right." She looked up at him. "She loves you."

"It's mutual," he replied. He smiled down at her, loving the softness in her green eyes. "We can add some more creature comforts for her, and fix what's wrong with the house."

"There's a lot wrong with it," she said worriedly.

"I'm rich, as you reminded me," he replied easily. "I can afford whatever she, and Selene, need. After all, they're family."

She hugged him warmly and laid her cheek against his chest. "Do you want to have kids?" she asked.

His eyebrows arched and his blue eyes twinkled. "Of course. Do you want to start them right now?" He looked around. "The kitchen table's just a bit short . . . ouch!"

She withdrew her fist from his stomach. "You know what I mean! Honestly, what am I going to do with you?"

"Want me to coach you?" he offered, and chuckled wickedly when she blushed.

"Look out that window and tell me what you see," she said.

He glanced around. There were people going in and out of the unfinished stable, working on the interior by portable lighting. There were a lot of people going in and out.

"I guarantee if you so much as kiss me, we'll be on every Internet social networking site in the world," she told him. "And not because of who you are."

He laughed out loud. “Okay. We’ll wait.” He glanced outside again and scowled. “But we are definitely not going to try to honeymoon here in this house!”

She didn’t argue.

He tugged her along with him into a dark hallway and pulled her close. “They’ll need night vision to see us here,” he explained as he bent to kiss her with blatant urgency.

She kissed him back, feeling so explosively hot inside that she thought she might burst. She felt shivery when he kissed her like that, with his mouth and his whole body. His hands smoothed up under her blouse and over her breasts. He felt the hard tips and groaned, kissing her even harder.

She knew nothing about intimacy, but she wanted it suddenly, desperately. She lifted up to him, trying to get even closer. He backed her into the wall and lowered his body against hers, increasing the urgency of the kiss until she groaned out loud and shivered.

The frantic little sound got through his whirling mind. He pushed away from her and stepped back, dragging in deep breaths in an effort to regain the control he’d almost lost.

“You’re stopping?” she asked breathlessly.

“Yes, I’m stopping,” he replied. He took her hand and pulled her back into the lighted kitchen. There was a flush along his high cheekbones. “Until the wedding, no more time alone,” he added huskily. His blue eyes met her green ones. "We're going to have it conventional, all the way. Okay?"

She smiled with her whole heart. "Okay!"

He laughed. "It's just as well," he sighed.

"Why?"

"We don't have a bed. Yet."

Her eyes twinkled. He was so much fun to be with, and when he kissed her, it was like fireworks. They were going to make a great marriage, she was sure of it. She stopped worrying about being poor. When they held each other, nothing mattered less than money.

But the next hurdle was the hardest. He announced a week later that his family was coming up to meet John's future bride. Sassy didn't sleep that night, worrying. What would they think, those fabulously wealthy people, when they saw where Sassy and her mother and Selene lived, how poor they were? Would they think she was only after John's wealth?

She was still worrying when they showed up at her front door late the next afternoon, with John. Sassy stood beside him in her best dress, as they walked up onto the front porch of the Peale home-place. Her best dress wasn't saying much because it was off the rack and two years old. It was long, beige, and simply cut. Her shoes were older than the dress and scuffed.

But the tall blond man and the slender, dark-haired woman didn't seem to notice or care how she was dressed. The woman, who didn't look much older than Sassy, hugged her warmly.

"I'm Kasie," she introduced herself with a big smile. "He's Gil, my husband." Gil smiled and shook her hand warmly. "And these are our babies . . ." She motioned to two little blond girls, one holding the other by the hand. "That's Bess," she said, smiling at the taller of the two, "and that's Jenny. Say hello! This is Uncle John's fiancée!"

Bess came forward and looked up at Sassy with wide, soft eyes. "You going to marry Uncle John? He's very nice."

"Yes, he is," Sassy said, sliding her hand into John's. "I promise I'll take very good care of him," she added with a smile.

"Okay," Bess said with a shy returning smile.

"Come on in," Sassy told them. "I'm sorry, it isn't much to look at . . ." she added, embarrassed.

"Sassy, we were raised by an uncle who hated material things," Gil told her gently. "We grew up in a place just like this, a rough country house. We like to think it gave us strength of character."

"What he means is, don't apologize," John said in a loud whisper.

She laughed when Gil and Kasie agreed. Later she would learn that Kasie had grown up in even rougher conditions, in a war zone in Africa with missionary parents who were killed there.

Mrs. Peale greeted them with Selene by her side, a little intimidated.

"Stop looking like that," John chided, and hugged her warmly. "This is my future little mother-in-law," he added with a grin, introducing her to his family. "She's the sweetest woman I've ever known, except for Kasie."

"You didn't say I was sweet, too," Sassy said with a mock pout.

"You're not sweet. You're precious," he told her with a warm, affectionate grin.

"Okay, I'll go with that," she laughed. She turned to the others. "Come in and sit down. I could make coffee . . . ?"

"Please, no," Gil groaned. "She pumped me full of it all the way here. We were up last night very late trying to put fences back up after a storm. Kasie had to drive most of the way." He held his stomach. "I don't think I ever want another cup."

"You go out with your men to fix fences?" Mrs. Peale asked, surprised.

"Of course," he said simply. "We always have."

Mrs. Peale relaxed. So did Sassy. These people were nothing like they'd expected. Even Selene warmed to them at once, as shy as she usually was with strangers. It was a wonderful visit.

"Well, what do you think of them?" John asked Sassy much later, as he was getting ready to leave for the ranch.

"They're wonderful," she replied, pressed close

against him on the dark porch. "They aren't snobs. I like them already."

"It's as Gil said," he replied. "We were raised by a rough and tumble uncle. He taught us that money wasn't the most important thing in life." He tilted her mouth up and kissed it. "They liked you, too," he added. He smiled. "So, no more hurdles. Now all we have to do is get married."

"But I don't know how to plan a big wedding," she said worriedly.

He grinned. "Not to worry. I know someone who does!"

The wedding was arranged beautifully by a consultant hired by John, out of Colorado. She was young and pretty and sweet, and apparently she was very discreet. Sassy was fascinated by some of the weddings she'd planned for people all over the country. One was that of Sassy's favorite country western singing star.

"You did that wedding?" Sassy exclaimed.

"I did. And nobody knew a thing about it until they were on their honeymoon," she added smugly. "That's why your future husband hired me. I'm the soul of discretion. Now, tell me what colors you like and we'll get to work!"

They ended up with a color scheme of pink and yellow and white. Sassy had planned a simple white gown, until Mary Garnett showed her a couture gown with the three pastels embroidered in silk into the bodice and echoed in the lace over the skirt, and in the veil. It was the most beautiful gown Sassy had ever seen in her life. "But you could buy a house for that!" Sassy exclaimed when she heard the price.

John, walking through the living room at the Peale house, paused in the doorway. "We're only getting married once," he reminded Sassy.

"But it's so expensive," she wailed.

He walked to the sofa and peered over her shoulder at the color photograph of the gown. His breath caught. "Buy it," he told Mary.

Sassy opened her mouth. He bent and kissed it shut. He walked out again.

Mary just grinned.

He had another surprise for her as well, tied up in a small box, as an early wedding present. He'd discovered that she'd had to pawn her grandfather's watch and pistol to pay bills and he'd gotten them out of hock. She cried like a baby. Which meant that he got to kiss the tears away. He was, she thought as she hugged him, the most thoughtful man in the whole world.

Sassy insisted on keeping her job, regardless of John's protests. She wanted to help more with the wedding, and felt guilty that she hadn't, but Mary had everything organized. Invitations were going out, flower arrangements were being made. A minister was engaged. A small orchestra was hired to play at the reception.

The wedding was being held at the family ranch in Medicine Ridge, to ensure privacy. Gil had already said that he was putting on more security for the event than the president of the United States had. Nobody was crashing this wedding. They'd even outfoxed aerial surveillance by putting the entire reception inside and having blinds on every window.

Nobody, he told John and Sassy, was getting in without an invitation and a photo ID.

"Is that really necessary?" Sassy asked John when they were alone.

"You don't know how well-known our parents are," he sighed. "They'll be coming, too, and our father can't keep his mouth shut. He's heard about you from Gil and Kasie, and he's bragging to anybody who'll listen about his newest daughter-in-law."

"Me?" She was stunned. "But I don't have any special skills and I'm not even beautiful."

John smiled down at her. "You have the biggest heart of any woman I've ever known," he said softly. "It isn't what you do or what you have that makes you special, Sassy. It's what you are."

She flushed. "What about your mother?"

He kissed her on the tip of her nose. "She's so happy to have access to her grandchildren, that she never raises a fuss about anything. But she's happy to have somebody in the family who can knit."

"How did you know I can knit?"

"You think I hadn't noticed all the afghans and chair covers and doilies all over your house?"

"Mama could have made them."

"But she didn't. She said you can even knit sweaters. Our mother would love to learn how. She wants you to teach her."

She caught her breath. "But, it's easy! Of course, I'll show her. She doesn't mind—neither of them minds—that I'm poor? They don't think I'm marrying you for your money?"

He laughed until his eyes teared up. "Sassy," he said, catching his breath, "you didn't know I had money until after I proposed."

"Oh."

"They know that, too."

She sighed. "Okay, then."

He bent and kissed her. "Only a few more days to go," he murmured. "I can hardly wait."

"Me, too," she said. "It's exciting. But it's a lot of work."

"Mary's doing the work so you don't have to. Well, except for getting the right dresses for your mother and Selene."

"That's not work," she laughed. "They love to shop. I'm so glad Mama's getting over the chemo. She's better every day. I was worried that she'd be too weak to come to the wedding, but she says she wouldn't miss it for anything."

"We'll have a nurse practitioner at the wedding," he assured her. "Just in case. Don't worry."

"I'll do my best," she promised.
"That's my girl."

Finally there was a wedding! Sassy had chewed her nails to the quick worrying about things going wrong. John assured her that it would be smooth as silk, but she couldn't relax. If only she didn't trip over her own train and go headfirst into the minister, or do something else equally clumsy! All those important people were going to be there, and she had stage fright.

But once she was at the door of the big ballroom at the Callister mansion in Medicine Ridge where the wedding was taking place, she was less nervous. The sight of John, in his tuxedo, standing at the altar, calmed her. She waited for the music and then, clutching her bouquet firmly, her veil in place over her face, she walked calmly down the aisle. Her heart raced like crazy as John turned and smiled down at her when she reached him. He was the most handsome man she'd ever seen in her life. And he was going to marry her!

The minister smiled at both of them and began the service. It was routine until he asked if John had the rings. John started fishing in his pockets and couldn't find them. He grimaced, stunned.

"Uncle John! Did you forget?" Jenny muttered at his side, shoving a silken pillow up toward him. "I got the rings, Uncle John!"

The audience chuckled. Sassy hid a smile.

John fumbled the rings loose from the pillow and bent and kissed his little niece on the forehead. "Thanks, squirt," he whispered.

She giggled and went to stand beside her sister, Bess, who was holding a basket full of fresh flower petals in shades of yellow, pink, and white.

The minister finished the ceremony and invited John to kiss his bride. John lifted the beautiful embroidered veil and pushed it back over Sassy's dark hair. His eyes searched hers. He framed her face in his big hands and bent and kissed her so tenderly that tears rolled down her cheeks, and he kissed every one away.

The music played again. Laughing, Sassy took the hand John held out and together they ran down the aisle and out the door. The reception was ready down the hall, in the big formal dining room that had been cleared of furniture for the occasion. As they ate cake and paused for photographs, to the strains of Debussy played by the orchestral ensemble, Sassy noticed movie stars, politicians, and at least two multimillionaires among the guests. She was rubbing elbows with people she'd only seen in magazines. It was fascinating.

"One more little hurdle, Mrs. Callister," John whispered to her, "and then we're going to Cancún for a week!"

"Sun and sand," she began breathlessly.

"And you and me. And a bed." He wiggled his eyebrows.

She laughed, pressing her face against him to hide her blushes.

"Well, it wasn't a bad wedding," came a familiar drawl from behind them.

Chief Graves was wearing a very nice suit, and nicely polished dress boots, holding a piece of cake on a plate. "But I don't like chocolate cake," he pointed out. "And there's no coffee."

"There is so coffee," John chuckled, holding up a cup of it. "I don't go to weddings that don't furnish coffee."

"Where did you get that?" he asked.

John nodded toward the far corner, where a coffee urn was half-hidden behind a bouquet of flowers.

Graves grinned. "I hope you have a long and happy life together."

"Thanks, Chief," Sassy told him.

"Glad you could make it," John seconded.

"I brought you a present," he said unexpectedly. He reached into his pocket and drew out a small package. "Something useful."

"Thank you," Sassy said, touched, as she took it from his hand.

He gave John a worldly look, chuckled, and walked off to find coffee.

"What is it, I wonder?" Sassy mused, tearing the paper open.

"Well!" John exclaimed when he saw what was inside.

She peered over his arm and smiled warmly. It was a double set of compact discs of romantic music and classical love themes.

They glanced toward the coffee urn. Graves lifted his cup and toasted them. They laughed and waved.

CHAPTER ELEVEN

THEY stayed on the beach in a hotel shaped like one of the traditional Maya pyramids. Sassy lay in John's strong arms still shivering with her first taste of intimacy, her face flushed, her eyes brilliant as they looked up into his.

"It gets better," he whispered as his mouth moved lightly over her soft lips. "First times are usually difficult."

"Difficult?" She propped up on one elbow. "Are we remembering the same first time? Gosh, I thought I was going to die!"

His blue eyes twinkled. "Forgive me. I naturally assumed from all the moaning and whimpering that you were . . . stop that!" He laughed when she pinched him.

An enthusiastic bout of wrestling followed.

He kissed her into limp submission. "We really must do this again, so that I can get my perspective back," he suggested. "I'll pay attention this time."

She laughed and kissed his broad shoulder. "See

that you do," she replied. She pushed him back into the pillows and followed him down.

"Now don't be rough with me, I'm fragile," he protested. "See here, take your hand off that . . . I'm not that sort of man!"

"Yes, you are," she chuckled, and put her mouth squarely against his. He was obediently silent for a long time afterward. Except for various involuntary sounds.

They held hands and walked down the beach at sunrise, watching seagulls soar above the incredible shades of blue that were the Gulf of Mexico.

"I never dreamed there were places like this," Sassy said dreamily. "The sand looks just like sugar."

"We'll have to take some postcards back with us. I can't believe I forgot to pack a digital camera," he sighed.

"We could buy one at the shop in the lobby," she suggested. "I have to have at least one picture of you in a bathing suit to put up in our house."

"Turnabout is fair play," he teased.

She laughed. "Okay."

"While we're at it, we'll buy presents for everybody."

"We should get something for Chief Graves."

"What would you suggest?"

"Something musical."

He pursed his lips. "We'll get him one of those wooden kazoos."

"No! Musical."

He drew her close. "Musical it is."

After the honeymoon, they stopped for the weekend at the Callister ranch in Medicine Ridge, where Sassy had time to sit down and get acquainted with John's sister-in-law, Kasie.

"I was so worried about fitting in here," Sassy confessed as they walked around the house, where the flowers were blooming in abundance around the huge swimming pool. "I mean, this is a whole world away from anything I know."

"I know exactly how you feel," Kasie said. "I was born in Africa, where my parents were missionaries," she recalled, going quiet. "They were killed right in front of us, me and my brother, Kantor. We went to live with our aunt in Arizona. Kantor grew up and married and had a little girl. He was doing a courier service by air in Africa when an attack came. He and his family were shot down in his plane and died." She sat down on one of the benches, her eyes far away. "I never expected to end up like this," she said, meeting the other girl's sympathetic gaze. "Gil didn't even like me at first," she added, laughing. "He made my life miserable when I first came to work here."

"He doesn't look like that sort of man," Sassy said. "He seems very nice."

"He can be. But he'd lost his first wife to a riding accident and he didn't ever want to get married again. He said I came up on his blind side. Of course, he thought I was much too young for him."

"Just like John," Sassy sighed. "He thought I was too young for him." She glanced at Kasie and grinned. "And I was sure that he was much too rich for me."

Kasie laughed. "I felt that way, too. But you know, it doesn't have much to do with money. It has to do with feelings and things you have in common." Her eyes had a dreamy, faraway look. "Sometimes Gil and I just sit and talk, for hours at a time. He's my best friend, as well as my husband."

"I feel that way with John," Sassy said. "He just fits in with my family, as if he's always known them."

"Mama Luke took to Gil right away, too." She noted the curious stare. "Oh, she's my mother's sister. She's a nun."

"Heavens!"

"My mother was pregnant with me and Kantor and a mercenary soldier saved her life," she explained. "His name was K.C. Kantor. My twin and I were both named for him."

"I've heard of him," Sassy said hesitantly, not liking to repeat what she'd heard about the reclusive, crusty millionaire.

"Most of what you've heard is probably true,"

Kasie laughed, seeing the words in her expression. "But I owe my life to him. He's a kind man. He would probably have married Mama Luke, if she hadn't felt called to a religious life."

"Is he married?"

Kasie frowned. "You know, I heard once that he did get married, to some awful woman, and divorced her right afterward. I don't know if it's true. You don't ask him those sort of questions," she added.

"I can understand why."

"Gil's parents like you," Kasie said out of the blue.

"They do?" Sassy was astonished. "But I hardly had time to say ten words to them at the wedding!"

"John said considerably more than ten words." Kasie grinned. "He was singing your praises long before he went back to marry you. Magdalena saw that beautiful shawl you'd packed and John told her you knitted it yourself. She wants to learn how."

"Yes, John said that, but I thought he was kidding!"

"She's not. She'll be in touch, I guarantee. She'll turn up at your ranch one of these days with her knitting gear and you'll have to chase her out with a broom."

Sassy blushed. "I'd never do that. She's so beautiful."

"Yes. She and the boys didn't even speak before

I married Gil. I convinced him to meet them on our honeymoon. He was shocked. You see, they were married very young and had children so early, long before they were ready for them. John and Gil's uncle took the boys to raise and sort of shut their parents out of their lives. It was a tragedy. They grew up thinking their parents didn't want them. It wasn't true. They just didn't know how to relate to their children, after all those years."

"I think parents and children need to be together those first few years," Sassy said.

"I agree wholeheartedly," Kasie said. She smiled. "Gil and I want children of our own, but we want the girls to feel secure with us first. There's no rush. We have years and years."

"The girls seem very happy."

Kasie nodded. "They're so much like my own children," she said softly. "I love them very much. I was heartbroken when Gil sent me home from Nassau and told me not to be here when they got home."

"What?"

Kasie laughed self-consciously. "We had a rocky romance. I'll have to tell you all about it one day. But for now, we'd better get back inside. Your husband will get all nervous and insecure if you're where he can't see you."

"He's a very nice husband."

"He's nice, period, like my Gil. We got lucky, for two penniless children, didn't we?" she asked.

Sassy linked her arm into Kasie's. "Yes, we did. But we'd both live in line cabins and sew clothes by hand if they asked us to."

"Isn't that the truth?" Kasie laughed.

"What were you two talking about for so long?" John asked that night, as Sassy lay close in his arms in bed.

"About what wonderful men we married," she said drowsily, reaching up to kiss him. "We did, too."

"Did Kasie tell you about her background?"

"She did. What an amazing story. And she said Gil didn't like her!"

"He didn't," he laughed. "He even fired her. But he realized his mistake in time. She was mysterious and he was determined not to risk his heart again."

"Sort of like you?" she murmured.

He laughed. "Sort of like me." He drew her closer and closed his eyes. "We go home tomorrow. Ready to take on a full-time husband, Mrs. Callister?"

"Ready and willing, Mr. Callister," she murmured, and smiled as she drifted off to sleep.

Several weeks later, Sassy had settled in at the ranch and was making enough knitted and crocheted accessories to make a home of the place. Mrs. Peale had a new companion, a practical nurse named Helen who was middle-aged, sweet, and could cook as well as clean house. She had no family, so Mrs. Peale and Selene filled an empty place in her life. Her charges were very happy with her. Sassy and John found time to visit regularly. They were like lovebirds, though. People rarely saw one without the other. Sassy mused that it was like they were joined at the hip. John grinned and kissed her for that. It was, indeed, he said happily.

One afternoon, John walked in the back door with Chief Graves, who was grinning from ear to ear.

"We have company," John told her, pausing to kiss her warmly and pull her close at his side. "He has news."

"I thought you'd like to know that Mr. Tarleton got five years," he said pleasantly. "They took him away last Friday. He's appealing, of course, but it won't help. He was recorded on DVD agreeing to the terms of the plea bargain. I told you that judge hated sexual assault cases."

Sassy nodded. "I'm sorry for him," she said. "I wish he'd learned his lesson the last time, in Wyoming. I guess when you do bad things for a long time, you just keep doing them."

"Repeat offenders repeat, sometimes," Graves replied solemnly. "But he's off the street, where he won't be hurting other young women." He pursed his lips. "I also wanted to thank you for the gift you brought back from Mexico. But I'm curious."

"About what?" she asked.

"How did you know I could play a flute?"

Her eyebrows arched. "You can?" she asked, surprised.

He chuckled. "Maybe she reads minds," he told John. "Better take good care of her. A woman with that rare gift is worth rubies."

"You're telling me," John replied, smiling down at his wife.

"I'll get back to town. Take care."

"You, too," Sassy said.

He sauntered out to his truck. John turned to Sassy with pursed lips. "So you can read minds, can you?" He leaned his forehead down against hers and linked his hands behind her. "Think you can tell me what I'm thinking right now?" he teased.

She reached up and whispered in his ear, grinning.

He laughed, picked her up, and stalked down the hall carrying her. She held on tight. Some men's minds, she thought wickedly, weren't all that difficult to read after all!

A prolific author of more than one hundred books, **Diana Palmer** got her start as a newspaper reporter. A multi-*New York Times* best-selling author and one of the top ten romance writers in America, she has a gift for telling the most sensual tales with charm and humor. Diana lives with her family in Cornelia, Georgia. Her hobbies include gardening, archaeology, anthropology, iguanas, astronomy and music. She has been married to James Kyle for over twenty-five years, and they have one son.

For news about Diana Palmer's latest releases, please visit www.dianapalmer.com.

Center Point Publishing
600 Brooks Road • PO Box 1
Thorndike ME 04986-0001 USA

(207) 568-3717

US & Canada:
1 800 929-9108
www.centerpointlargeprint.com